EDENDERRY

1 5 JUN 2022

WITHDRAWN

C

## SPECIAL MESSAGE TO READERS

**THE ULVERSCROFT FOUNDATION**
**(registered UK charity number 264873)**
was established in 1972 to provide funds for
research, diagnosis and treatment of eye diseases.
Examples of major projects funded by
the Ulverscroft Foundation are:-

- The Children's Eye Unit at Moorfields Eye Hospital, London
- The Ulverscroft Children's Eye Unit at Great Ormond Street Hospital for Sick Children
- Funding research into eye diseases and treatment at the Department of Ophthalmology, University of Leicester
- The Ulverscroft Vision Research Group, Institute of Child Health
- Twin operating theatres at the Western Ophthalmic Hospital, London
- The Chair of Ophthalmology at the Royal Australian College of Ophthalmologists

You can help further the work of the Foundation
by making a donation or leaving a legacy.
Every contribution is gratefully received. If you
would like to help support the Foundation or
require further information, please contact:

**THE ULVERSCROFT FOUNDATION**
**The Green, Bradgate Road, Anstey**
**Leicester LE7 7FU, England**
**Tel: (0116) 236 4325**

**website: www.foundation.ulverscroft.com**

# HANDLE WITH CARE

Why is Leo Dryden so reluctant to explain to his daughter Jess the mystery surrounding her mother's death? Who is the charismatic Lucas, suddenly arriving with dramatic news? When Leo is rushed into hospital, Jess is left to face unforeseen dangers. Is the helpful Oliver all he seems? And then there is Sam, arriving alone in Leeds on a quest to find her beloved boyfriend Nat. But Lucas is involved with her too . . .

*Books by Anne Hewland*
*in the Linford Romance Library:*

ANNE HEWLAND

# HANDLE WITH CARE

*Complete and Unabridged*

## LINFORD
*Leicester*

First published in Great Britain in 2015

First Linford Edition
published 2016

Copyright © 2015 by Anne Hewland
All rights reserved

A catalogue record for this book is available
from the British Library.

ISBN 978–1–4448–2983–9

Published by
F. A. Thorpe (Publishing)
Anstey, Leicestershire

Set by Words & Graphics Ltd.
Anstey, Leicestershire
Printed and bound in Great Britain by
T. J. International Ltd., Padstow, Cornwall

This book is printed on acid-free paper

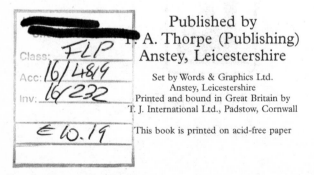
Class: FLP
Acc: 16/4849
16/232
Inv: 16/232
€ 10.19

# 1

They stood together, looking down at the discreet grey marble headstone. The question caught in her throat. Jess swallowed and began again. 'How did my mother die?'

Would her father give her the answer at last, after fobbing her off for so long? Over the last fortnight, she had sensed a change in him, a feeling of suppressed excitement. Ever since she had opened his door to the young man with dark hair and an engaging grin. Had he brought news of some kind? If so, her father hadn't seemed willing to share it.

She couldn't forget it — or him. But for the next day or two, Jess hadn't referred to it, until some instinct had made her say, 'Was that message something to do with my mother? Are you ready to tell me about her now?'

'Yes,' her father had said slowly. 'I

1

think I may be. Very soon.'

When Jess had next gone round, she had caught him looking at her carefully, as if considering something. And now he had kept his promise. Her father had hired a cottage for a couple of days and brought her to this small village in Leicestershire.

Jess was staring at the name, drinking it in. *Dryden. In memory of a beloved wife and mother.* She said, half to herself, 'Wasn't her name Carolyn?'

Her father was silent.

'Dad?' She turned and looked up at him. The silence had gone on too long. His face was blank. Slowly, one hand crept to his chest.

He said in a low voice, 'Think I shall have to sit down.'

'Are you all right?' Stupid question, when obviously he wasn't.

'Don't worry.' He was lowering himself onto a tomb slab, slowly and deliberately. Surely he couldn't be having a heart attack? No, it didn't seem dramatic enough. He would be fine in a minute.

She scanned his face, hoping the colour would return. But he had been pale that morning anyway — and on edge. Not surprising, considering where they were going. She shouldn't have kept on at him.

Her fingers were already searching for her phone. 'I'll ring 999.' Expecting him to say, 'No, I'm okay now. Just a blip.' He never liked fuss.

He said, 'Perhaps that would be best.'

Jess dialled, and pressed the phone to her ear.

'What service do you require?' enquired the calm voice of the operator.

She answered automatically, responding to the questions. 'I don't know where we are.'

Her father told her the name of the village. She repeated it without taking it in.

'The new cemetery. Just across from the parish church,' her father said. He closed his eyes.

'Dad, stay with me. Please. They're on their way.'

He smiled. 'I know. It's okay. I'm just feeling a bit tired.'

There was moisture on his forehead. His breathing seemed slow and shallow. What should she do? Chest compression? But he was still conscious. She couldn't remember . . .

He opened his eyes again. 'Don't worry. I'll be okay.'

If he was still talking to her, that could be true. She was hoping desperately that it was. 'Are you feeling any better?'

'Not really. The pain's still there. In my chest and along my arm.'

Out on the road, she heard a car pass. She stood up. Could they even be seen in here, surrounded by the implacable headstones? She looked round. Where was the ambulance? How long ago had she rung them? She looked at her watch. Time seemed to have stopped. Should she try ringing again?

No, of course not. They would be doing their best. She'd given them all the information. Everything her father had told her. They would know how important it was. They would have a satnav. They would know the area better than she did.

Another vehicle — and this time, thank goodness, the welcome beacon of the green and yellow of the paramedics. Not a full-size ambulance. By now, she hardly cared. 'They're here, Dad. I'll run and get them. Wait here.'

Another stupid thing to say. But a relief to be handing the responsibility over to someone else. The team in their dark green overalls with their metallic cases of equipment were calm, unhurried and efficient. She thought, listening to their questions about the nature of the pain, that perhaps it would all turn out to have been a mistake. On a scale of one to ten, how bad was it? Seven, her father thought. Eight, maybe.

They couldn't see anything definitely wrong with his heart, according to their readings. His blood pressure was higher than they would like. They had given him something for the pain. On a scale of one to ten? He wasn't sure. Six?

Jess thought, *I'm not really here.* Everything was happening without her. Any minute, he would shake his head, smile, and say the pain had gone. Now they were asking for a backup ambulance which had further to come. More waiting. Another team.

Numb, she climbed up the metal step after the stretcher. It seemed to be expected of her. She didn't question that. 'Where are we going?' A hospital she had never heard of. She didn't know Leicestershire. Did her father know it? She supposed he must do, or had once.

This new paramedic was capable and calming. Jess hardly noticed what she was doing. Or how her father was responding. On a scale of one to ten? Her senses were dulled. She looked hopelessly out of the windows as green fields and trees flashed past. No landmarks. Nothing to tell her where they were going. Not as if she had even known for definite where they had started from. She sat there, letting this happen. What else was there to do?

Urban landscape now. Buildings and traffic. 'Nothing to panic about, but we're going to put the siren on to get through this lot.'

Arrival. Wheeling the stretcher along a corridor. In a queue of trolleys. The two paramedics, her new friends, were leaving. She wanted to cling on to them. Gone. She couldn't tell how long the queue was; the corridor curved away in front of them. She looked back to study the people behind them: the man in the first trolley was covered in blood. She turned back quickly.

Somebody came to fill in a form. Went away again. Eventually from the trolley to a bed, with curtains. Progress. Somebody else, to fill in what seemed like the same form. More waiting.

Her father said, 'You should go. What time is it?'

'Not yet. I'll wait until you see a doctor. I want to see which ward you go to.'

'No, Jess. You've seen the news reports on A&E these days, surely? I

7

could be here for hours. Days, even.' He grinned and then winced. 'Come back tomorrow.'

'No way.'

More waiting. Her father started to move his arms and legs, restlessly.

'Are you okay? Shall I fetch someone?'

'No, I'm fine. No worse, anyhow. Look, Jess, I'm worried about *you* now.'

'Nobody seems to mind me staying here.'

'It's not a good idea.' He paused. 'There's something you need to know.' He stopped, his eyes sliding away. 'There's someone looking for me.'

'What? Who?'

'An old business partner, that's all. Let's say we didn't see eye to eye. We parted — less than amicably.'

'You shouldn't be telling me this. Not now.' After all the trauma and worry of what must be a heart attack, this old business partner, whoever he was, hardly seemed important. She couldn't take it in. 'You mustn't get stressed.'

He had a stubborn look. 'I have to tell you. I'm thinking about you.'

'But how can it affect me? I've never heard you mention this before. It's nothing to do with me.' She frowned. 'Is it?'

He said quickly, 'Of course not. But he may want to make contact with me.'

'Not if you're in here. Just concentrate on getting better. Please.'

'I mean, if I'm stuck here and you go home ... Best if you don't tell him where I am.'

'Of course not. I won't tell anyone. Not if you don't want me to.'

'And don't go back to Yorkshire yet. Wait for me.'

'I wasn't going to. I wouldn't, would I? We've got the cottage for the next three days, haven't we? I'll stay there.' She thought, *If I know where it is from here. If I know where I am.*

He seemed to know what she was thinking. 'Don't worry, you can get a taxi.'

'Yes, of course I can. No problem. Don't worry about me.'

'There are always taxis outside the main door here. The main door, mind. Not where we came in. Just follow the signs. You'll be sure to find one there. Just give the driver the address of the cottage, and he'll look after you.' He felt in his pocket. 'Here, this is the address.' He smiled. 'I knew you'd forgotten it.'

'I don't think I ever knew it.'

'You have it now.'

'Okay.' Jess managed a smile. 'Don't worry about a thing, Dad. You're in the best place and they'll sort you out. You may even be able to leave tomorrow morning, when we have the test results.'

He returned a strained smile. 'Of course. Sorry to be such a pain with all this. Spoiling things. I know this was important to you. I'll make it up to you.'

'Not your fault.' She tried to sound brisk and matter-of-fact. 'Okay, then. See you tomorrow.'

She walked quickly away, turning as she reached the corridor. Through a gap in the curtains, she saw him lying back on his pillow, eyes closed. He looked so drained and ill, now that he was no longer trying to make an effort — for her.

She took a wrong turn somehow and then another. She was certain she had been following Way Out signs. Where was this Main Entrance with the taxis? It would be so much better when she had retrieved the car. She swore gently. She didn't know where that was either, not in relation to Leicester. It was back near the church where she had phoned for the ambulance.

Should she get the taxi driver to find the car first? No, it would be dark soon. She could hardly ask him to drive round looking for a village she couldn't now remember the name of. Just go back to the cottage. Begin again in the morning.

At last. What must be a reception area with a woman behind a glass screen and people waiting. Beyond that, the doors. Thank goodness for that. She walked out into a covered drop-off area.

Not a great deal of room for taxis, but there was one, just off to her left, with the firm's name on the door. That was lucky.

She bent down to the window without troubling to look at the driver's face, and showed him the piece of paper. 'Here, please. How far is it? How much will it be?'

He was wearing a cap, pulled forward over his eyes. 'Fifteen pounds, love.'

Jess frowned, trying to remember whether she had enough. Yes, she was certain she had two twenties, at least. She remembered going to a cash machine before meeting her father in Leeds the day before. How long ago that seemed. 'Yes, thanks. That will be fine.'

She slid into the back seat. This time, she must take notice of where they were going, for when she drove back tomorrow. She didn't like the feeling of not knowing where she was. Too disorientating. Satnavs were good, but she liked to feel in control.

They came out onto the road and were surrounded by the blank brick walls of buildings that all looked the same. What did she know about Leicester? Richard III, of course, and that was it.

They must be moving out of the city centre by now. Jess had lost all sense of distance. If he was charging £15 at so much per mile, surely she could work it out . . . Her brain wasn't functioning properly. Shock, maybe. She gave it up as the miles passed.

Surely they should be somewhere near by now? She hadn't even glimpsed a road sign for some time. They were driving down a narrow lane with grass down the middle. Their cottage had been set back a little from a B road. No need for a lane like this, which was now little more than a track.

She leaned forward. 'Excuse me. Are you sure this is right?'

'It's what the satnav's telling me.' He spoke over his shoulder. 'But it can't be far now. Don't you recognise this?'

'Not at all. And the satnav may be wrong.'

He nodded. 'Do you want to go back to where we turned off?'

'Maybe we should.' Why was this happening? She felt as if she'd gone from one nightmare into another. And for someone who prided herself on efficiency, she didn't seem to be at all capable of deciding anything. She just wanted to get back to the cottage, have something to eat, ring the hospital and make a plan for the following day.

'Sorry, love.' The man sounded too cheerful to be sorry. 'It must have freaked out again. I'll turn in this gateway. And don't worry, I'll stick to the original quote.'

'Good. Thanks.' Idiot. What was she thanking him for, when this was his fault? She was glad she had rejected the idea of getting him to look for the car. No way.

They were lurching forward now, over what felt like a pile of stones. The car juddered to a halt. He tried to

14

reverse. Nothing happened.

Jess said, 'We're stuck on something. Perhaps you should get out and try and shift it. Whatever it is.'

'Good idea.' He got out and was bending forwards, obviously examining the wheels. Jess turned to look out of the rear window. They were vulnerable in this position, if a farm vehicle or something came hurtling along. But at least they could ask for directions. Might even be able to grab a lift . . .

No chance. Nothing and no one in sight.

He opened his door again. 'I can see it now. If you get out, it should be just enough to lift us. It's not stuck by much.'

Jess sighed. 'Let's hope so.' She stepped out, looking down at what she might be treading on — or into. And suddenly, something dark was over her head and her wrists were being pulled behind her and she was being pushed and pulled sideways and down.

A hard shove to her back, and she fell

into what must be the car boot. It had all been so sudden. She could hardly breathe. Her hands were being hastily bound.

She heard the lid slam over her head and the doors shutting before the taxi reversed with no problem at all.

She lay frozen with terror, her head muzzy from hitting the hard floor of the boot. What was happening?

# 2

Sam reached for her phone, checking the screen. 'Are you okay, Mum? Is something wrong?'

Her mother was trying too hard to sound brisk and breezy. 'Of course not. Sorry to ring you at work. Just thought I'd better let you know that I'm moving.'

'You never said.' Sam tried not to sound reproachful. 'I've only been gone a week or two.' But her neck was prickling. *Not again.* As a child, this had happened so many times. They would be rushing off in the dark, leaving all her friends behind. Once, even her favourite fluffy blue rabbit.

'Well, the place seemed too big without you. And you're happily settled with your new job and new flat. And I've been travelling around a lot with my job anyway. Better to get somewhere nearer to work. And we were in Lambeth for

17

ages, weren't we?'

*Were?* 'Have you gone already?'

Of course she had. Sam sighed.

'Don't worry about your things. I packed very carefully. I have them all here.' That bright voice again.

Sam wished she'd never moved out. But if she hadn't come up to Leeds, how could she ever trace Nat? Except that, so far, there had been no sign of him. 'Where are you? I need your address.'

'I'll phone again when you're on your own. But I had to let you know straight away, just in case you needed to contact me. And Sam, take a note of this phone number. I'm not using the old one now.'

Sam rested her head on one hand. There was real fear in her mother's voice. Perhaps there had been every time they moved. Trying to make everything seem fun — but Sam had always picked up on the underlying tension.

'Are you okay? Please tell me.'

'Everything's fine, now I'm here. Don't worry about me.'

'I can come back.'

'No.' Her mother's voice was sharp. 'Stay where you are. That will be best.' She paused. 'Just — be careful.'

'About what?'

'No, you know me. I'm being paranoid now. Always imagining things. And the stress of my little girl leaving home. You'll be fine where you are. I'm sure of that. Bye, now.'

Sam put the phone down and looked cautiously round the office. Be careful of what? Was it all starting again? They had seemed so quiet and settled for the last few years, while she had attended sixth-form college and university.

Across the desk, Claire was smiling at her, eyes wide and curious. 'Who was that? Not that mysterious man you've been looking for, at long last?'

'My mum.'

'Ah.' Claire nodded.

Sam bit her lips together. Perhaps she shouldn't even have said that. She could easily have let Claire think it *had* been Nat.

'Come on,' Claire said. 'Admit it.

That wasn't your mum at all. If it wasn't that Nat person, it'll be one of the others. More than likely — because, I meant to tell you, that dark dishy one is out there now *again*, waiting for you to finish. How many times this week? I wish I was in such demand.'

Sam sighed. 'Oh dear.'

'Shall I tell him to go away? I can say you've already gone. And then you can nip out the back way again.'

No doubt Claire was trying to be helpful and sympathetic but Sam suspected that she was enjoying this mini-drama. Probably Claire's existence was very dull and bland, and any excitement, even in someone else's life, would be welcomed. She was always complaining about how boring this job was, and how her art and design abilities were lying dormant. For a moment, Sam was tempted to take up the offer and escape.

She shook her head. 'No, it's okay. It will only be putting things off.'

'Suppose. So, what is it with him? You dumped him back in London and

20

he just can't get it, is that it? And he's tracked you down here. Is he stalking you?'

'No. He dumped *me*. Last year.'

'Oh!' Claire paused, thinking. 'And now he's realised he's made a big mistake. Were you upset when it happened?'

'Devastated,' Sam said.

'And of course you'll get back together, but you want him to suffer first. I would.'

'No. Now there's Nat.' Or there should be, if only she knew where he'd gone.

'And I know you go for older men, too, don't you? I don't blame you. Much more likely to be rich and successful.'

Sam frowned. 'I don't know what you mean.' She didn't want to bother with any of this. Not now. She was too worried about her mother. She didn't want to be explaining everything to Claire, and she didn't want to bother with Lucas, either.

Or did she? She stared unseeing at her screen while Claire prattled on. Lucas had known her mother. Sam's mother had always been suspicious of her boyfriends, but amazingly, Lucas had won her round. And he knew about Sam's unsettled childhood and how they'd moved about so much. She hadn't told him about the abruptness, the fear of not knowing where they were going or why — but she hadn't needed to. Lucas could be perceptive; he'd picked up on that somehow. Perhaps talking to him would be a good idea. He would understand.

High time, also, to tell him about her search for Nat, and how Lucas could never, ever now regain that place in her heart. If he was willing to be just a friend, fair enough. Perhaps he would be okay with that.

Claire was saying, 'Would you like some back-up? Shall I come out with you? He seems a bit creepy to me. In a sinister kind of way. Though he's very good-looking.'

'What? Oh, no, thanks. I'll be fine, honestly.'

Claire looked disappointed — petulant, even — before she smiled and nodded. 'Well, I'm off now, anyway.'

Sam leaned forward. 'I do appreciate your support. But I think I'll be better on my own.'

'Okay. See you tomorrow.'

Sam shut down her screen, feeling almost guilty at the relief she felt as Claire went out. She was only trying to be kind, wasn't she? It wasn't her fault Sam's life was in a muddle. She put on her coat, slowly, giving her colleague time to get going.

As she stepped out onto the street, Lucas was staring into the distance. Sam smiled, knowing he was completely aware of her. She'd always teased him about the way he did that. She thought it was so the person approaching could admire his profile.

He turned at exactly the right time, as she'd known he would. 'Hello, Sam.'

'Hello, Lucas.'

'I was just passing. Fancy a drink on the way home?'

'No, you weren't. And no thanks, I don't.'

'I made you smile, though. How about something to eat, then? You're later than usual.'

She shook her head and then paused. Perhaps it would be better explaining about Nat at length, sitting down somewhere. And then there was Mum . . .

'Saves you cooking for yourself.'

'Okay, then. Only because I do need to talk to you. Equal shares.'

'Of course. No obligation.' He lifted his phone. 'I'd just like to confirm my booking for two, please. About fifteen minutes.'

'Lucas!' She shook her head. 'You didn't know I'd come.'

He grinned. 'Really? Anyhow, you'll like this place. Guaranteed.'

'If you say so.' She should have made more of a fuss, but just now, she was too worried to care. Just let him get on with it.

He led the way to a restaurant with a Victorian frontage, facing onto the square near the train station. Sam was thinking, planning what she was going to say. She'd forgotten how easily Lucas could distract you. He murmured to the waiter and they were shown to a table by the window. It was still early for eating; there were at least a dozen tables available.

She said, 'I'm surprised you needed to book. Oh, I see. You didn't, did you?'

That grin again. 'Maybe not.'

Better get the food out of the way. Sam scanned the menu. She didn't feel particularly hungry. Perhaps a drink would have been better, after all. But she needed a clear head or he would run rings round her.

'I'll have the salmon, please.'

'Good choice. I'll have the same.' The waiter moved away and Lucas leaned forward, smiling into her eyes. 'I'm glad you agreed to come. I've been looking forward to showing you round Leeds, ever since I first realised you were here.'

Sam said quickly, 'We're not going to start up again from where we left off, you know.'

'No. You made that clear already. And

I wouldn't expect to. Our parting was my fault, I admit that. My mistake.'

'No. Because that was over a year ago, and I'm committed to someone else now.'

Lucas raised his eyebrows. 'You are? Congratulations. So where is he?'

'Ah, he's in Leeds too. Or he was. To begin with.' In a moment, she would be admitting she had no idea where Nat was, and that he didn't even know she was here. 'He worked for the same firm as I do, in London.' Should she pretend he was temporarily in a different office? No, Lucas would see right through her. And what did that matter? Lucas would just have to believe her on this.

Lucas didn't seem surprised. 'But you haven't caught up with him yet.' It wasn't a question. 'No worries. We can be mates while we're waiting for you to sort yourself out.'

'Whether I sort things out or not?'

'Whatever. Come on, Sam. I know you too well and I can see you're in need of a friend. A real friend, with your best interests at heart, not that girl who tried to pretend you'd already left the other night. You're such a happy person. And right now, you're not happy.'

There was a lump in Sam's throat. 'I'm fine.'

'This new man you're looking for; would his name be Nat?'

'How did you know?' She felt a surge of hope. 'Do you know him? Do you know where he is?'

'I'm afraid not. But I know his name because your mother told me.'

'Mum? When did you speak to *her*? Was she all right?'

'Yes, of course. Why wouldn't she be?' He hadn't moved, and yet she sensed that he was suddenly tense. 'I thought I'd caught sight of you, on the Headrow last week, and I phoned her to check.'

'And she told you?'

'Naturally. Your mum always liked me.' He paused, staring at her. 'I'm afraid she didn't seem too keen on this Nat.'

'She's never met him. And that

wasn't his fault. Mum can be difficult with new boyfriends, you know that.'

'She didn't like the way he upset you, when he just disappeared like that. She didn't seem too happy either that you'd got that temporary transfer to the office up here. Rushing off to somewhere where you didn't know anyone. She was relieved to hear I was here.'

'I know all that. And it may have been a bit sudden, but I had to try.'

He was scanning her face closely. 'No, he isn't the whole problem, is he? There's something else.'

Sam took a breath and found herself telling him. 'It's Mum. Everything was fine a week ago when you spoke to her, but she's moved again. And I don't know where she's gone. Or why. She rang me at work and wouldn't say. She said she'd get back to me.'

'Ah.' Lucas thought for a moment or two, turning his knife and fork over. 'You've always moved around a lot, though. That's what you told me. I'm sure she'll be fine. She's independent.

Resourceful. That's your mum.'

Sam wound a strand of her long, fair hair round her fingers. 'She told me to be careful.'

'Mothers always say that.' But his face was wary rather than reassuring.

'No. She meant it. I could tell by her voice.'

'What do you think she meant?'

'I don't know.' Sam frowned. If her mother had known Lucas was here, why hadn't she said something? Why hadn't she told Sam Lucas could help her with settling in, getting to know people, all the sort of things her mother had been concerned about? What if it was Lucas she had to be careful of? She felt cold suddenly.

Lucas put a hand over hers. 'Don't worry. She'll be fine. She just needs time to settle in and then she'll ring with the new address. And I'm here to look out for you. She knows that.' He grinned again. 'As a friend.'

'Thanks.' That reassurance should have helped, but now she was no longer sure. About anything.

The food arrived and she poked it around on the plate, wishing she hadn't bothered. She should have gone straight home. If her mother rang again, how could she talk to her here? Particularly if she had unwittingly come out with the person her mother was warning her about? But Mum should have said, in that case.

Sam sighed. Her mother had always been so secretive and self-contained. 'I'm sorry I'm not very good company. But I needed to explain. And I don't want you hanging around outside the office every night. Please.'

'No problem. Now we've made contact, I can text you. Ignore me if you like. But I'm glad we've been able to talk about this. For now, you need a friend, and I'm here to listen. And seriously, I know you and your mother moved around a lot — and I'll bet it was sudden more often than not. As a kid, you probably just didn't notice.'

'Maybe.' Sam smiled half-heartedly.

He was trying to help, but if she started comparing past moves, she would be more worried than ever. She'd only been concerned with changing schools and making new friends. And it had only ever happened in the holidays — hadn't it? She wasn't certain now. Forget it.

'I haven't asked about you. What brought you to Leeds?'

'Work,' he said. The usual thing. Northern expansion within his field. Sam was listening politely, but was getting the feeling that he was no longer concentrating on what he was saying. His eyes were focussing on the other side of the room.

Sam gave up on the salmon and sat back.

Lucas said, 'I've just spotted someone I need to speak to. That okay? You don't mind?'

'Go ahead.' He was on his feet before she answered. Just like him. Always too many things going on at once. But now that didn't matter. She turned idly, watching him cross the room and greet a man with short, dark hair and a narrow face. As Lucas sat down, the man turned and looked straight at her.

She frowned, looking away. It had been almost as if the stranger thought he knew her, but she didn't recognise him at all. She turned back to face the window looking out onto the square.

Amongst the scattering of anonymous figures crossing the paved area, one was suddenly achingly familiar. She was frozen to her chair, her stomach wrenching. Yes, it had to be. The way he was walking; the way he held his head. Everything about him.

Without thought, she ran out through the heavy glass doors and down the steps, ignoring the cold as she pelted after him. She could have shouted to him, but something stopped her. Her voice would be lost in the space. Wait until she was closer. Much closer.

She had acted quickly — but not fast enough. Already he was waiting at the lights on the far side of the square.

Glowing red in the distance, like a beacon. Light glancing on the cars turning the corner. She was almost there. Another few steps and she could touch him.

Now she called to him. 'Nat!' Her voice was barely audible above the roar of the traffic as she was panting so hard. But he heard her. He turned. And for one joyful moment, his face was alight with pleasure.

'Sam!' And then his face closed against her as if a shutter had come down between them. 'What are you doing here?' His voice was wary.

'I've got a new job. Here. I only started a couple of weeks ago.'

'You shouldn't have come. It's not — ' He stopped.

Sam stared at him. Had he been going to say 'safe'? First her mum, and now him. 'I don't know what you mean.'

'No, of course you don't. It doesn't matter.' He glanced back over the expanse of space where the fountains rose and fell, as if looking for something. Or some-one.

She said, miserably, 'Look, I can see you're in a hurry right now. I'm sorry I stopped you. I mean, can I see you later?'

From across the square, she could hear someone calling her name. Oh, no. Not now. Ignore him. Nat's head shot round. Before she knew what was happening, he was taking her hand in his. A tingling feeling shot up her arm. She had so wanted to feel his touch, just once more. But not like this.

'Sam!' The voice was nearer now, as if Lucas was running towards them.

Nat put his face close to her ear. 'Don't say anything about me. Please. This is important.'

She gulped. 'Yes, of course. If that's what you want.'

'Thanks.' He smiled at last, dropping her hand, looking behind her so that automatically she turned, following the direction of his gaze. Lucas was now only yards away. She turned back, thinking to warn Nat — and he was across the road, dodging through the moving traffic.

A large blue lorry trundled between them, and when it passed, he had gone.

# 3

Bumping along in the dark, Jess lost all track of time passing. Terror, pain, discomfort. What was happening? Where were they going? She must have knocked her head as she was tumbled into the boot, because she was drifting in and out of consciousness.

Was he going to kill her? But if so, why bother taking her somewhere else? They had been in a lonely enough spot in the first place. The same thinking could apply to robbery. Each time she woke, in the dark, there was the constant vibration shaking through her body. At least she could breathe; the boot wasn't airtight. Be thankful for that — if she could be grateful for anything.

And what about her dad? How could she get back to see him? And then — was this what he had been warning her against? The excitement she'd noticed over the past few days; was that part of it? When that dark, very good-looking man had come to the house last week . . . Her father employed more people than she could keep tabs on in the small but lucrative businesses he dealt with and managed, and his employees weren't usually encouraged to come to the house.

She had only just happened to be there with some figures her father needed. Happened to open the door. The stranger had said, 'I think he'll see me,' with that memorable grin.

Leo Dryden had come out into the hall. 'Lucas! Is there news?'

'Yes. And just what you wanted to hear.'

'Good man.' A pat on the back as her father ushered Lucas into his study, closing the door.

Jess didn't hear him leave, but her father was glowing, rubbing his hands together. She didn't ask what it had been about. If he wanted her to know, he would tell her. She said instead, 'Gone already? I was hoping you might introduce us.'

'Sorry, Jess.' He laughed. 'He's in a relationship at present.'

'Only at present?'

'No go. Hands off, Jess.' That brief memory of distant happiness, piercing her fear.

She drifted off again.

Woke with her head throbbing, but feeling more alert. Time to start thinking. She wriggled her hands. The bindings weren't tight; he hadn't even tied her properly. Inefficient — or was that what he'd intended? Whichever, it gave her a purpose. Something to do. She would not just lie here, a passive victim.

Take it slowly, don't do anything in a panic. Yes, her hands were free. Now to tackle the bag over her head. Easy, it wasn't fastened at all. She pulled it off, shaking her dark hair free, brushing strands of sacking from her face. Taking in great gasps of relatively clean air.

Exhausted with the effort, she must have dozed off again.

The next time she woke, the car was

blessedly still. She listened. No sounds. And the boot was not completely dark. The carpet must be torn, or missing, in places. That was why she'd been able to breathe from the start, even through the sacking.

In fact, as she put her face close to the source of the draught, she could glimpse daylight. She must have been locked in here all night. Still no sound of anyone outside. No traffic. So where was she? And how could she get out?

Her legs were stiff; she tried moving them, twisting her feet to alleviate the cramp. Stretching her arms as far as she could, before pushing against the metal above her. It didn't move. Was there anything useful in the boot with her?

She felt around with her fingers. An empty crisp packet, which made her realise how hungry she was. An odd glove. Surely there must be something else? Where were the tools for changing the tyres? No sign of anything. The spare tyre would be accessed from underneath. She lifted the carpet, one corner at a time. Yes, here was something. She delved into the gap and found a small spanner.

She clutched it in triumph. A weapon, maybe. Or she could use it to open the boot. Or find any weak spots and make a hole.

Was he still here? She listened intently. Hoping to hear a movement, a cough. Nothing. In the distance there was perhaps the murmur of traffic passing. Had the driver abandoned the car — and her? If so, she could use the spanner to make a noise and attract attention.

She gripped the spanner and banged on the lid. No, better to try SOS in Morse. Which came first, long or short? And did that matter? More importantly, if her abductor was still around, he would have rushed to silence her. And that hadn't happened. So she could carry on and hope someone was passing and would hear her.

She started again, getting into a rhythm. Gritting her teeth against the reverberation of the noise in the confined space.

Pausing every so often to listen, through the ringing in her ears. Nothing. It was no good. Her arms were aching and she could hardly grip the spanner. She put her head down in despair.

When the boot was flung open, it shocked her. Blinding light flooded over her. She was forced to close her eyes.

Someone said, 'Good grief! Are you all right?'

Stupidly, she squeaked, 'Yes, fine.' She squinted up at the figure towering over her, silhouetted against the sun.

He grasped her arm, gently but firmly. His voice was warm and concerned. 'Let's get you out of there.'

She wanted to say she could manage, thanks, but without her saviour's strong grip, her legs would have given way. Her arms and hands were shaking. Fortunate that she hadn't been faced with the kidnapper; she doubted whether she could have summoned up enough strength to hit him.

'Don't try to say anything yet.' He was passing her a bottle of water.

She unscrewed the top and gulped gratefully. She tried to speak, gasped and spluttered, and began again. 'I have to go to the hospital in Leicester. I have to find my father.'

His eyes widened. 'Your father? Has he been in an accident?'

How could she expect him to make sense of any of it? 'Sorry. I think he may have had a heart attack. I got a taxi from the hospital last night, and the driver attacked me and locked me in. What time is it?'

The man was saying, 'This isn't a taxi.'

She looked at her watch. 'I have to get to the hospital. What? It is a taxi. It has a name on the side.'

'Not now, it doesn't. Don't worry, I'll drive you.'

Jess hesitated. Could she trust him? No good had come from getting into what she'd thought was a genuine taxi, and this man was a complete stranger. But what option did she have? And he *had* let her out.

She frowned, assessing him. There

seemed to be something familiar and reassuring about him. Although when she looked at him more closely — dark hair, light eyes, narrow face — she couldn't say what that was. Had they met before somewhere?

He was waiting for her to make up her mind, half-smiling. Not hassling her.

'Yes, okay then. Thanks. Do you know where it is?'

'I have a fair idea. And a satnav.'

'Yes, of course. I don't know the postcode.'

'My car's just here.' He had pulled up a few yards away.

'Oh, my bag. It was on the floor, in the back.' She shook her head. 'I don't suppose it is now.' That must have been the motive. Robbery.

'Yes, here it is.' He paused, obviously picking up on her disbelief. 'Perhaps he didn't notice it.'

'Wow. Lucky.' She checked it quickly. Phone. Purse. Keys. Amazing. Thank goodness for that. But no text messages. Surely Dad would be worried sick by now. Wondering wherever she'd got to.

She got in beside him while he looked for the postcode on his phone. She said, 'The taxi driver was supposed to be taking me to our holiday cottage. We were staying there for a few days.'

'There we go.' He swung round, avoiding the car that had been her prison for all those hours. Jess shuddered. 'So, after you've seen your father and found out what the diagnosis is, I could give you a lift back there. Both of you, if necessary.'

'I can't be taking up your time like this. And we can easily get a — ' She stopped.

'I'm sure you'd be fine with a taxi next time. The receptionist would give you the number of a taxi firm. There's no rank at the main entrance.'

That was odd. The driver must have been waiting for *her*. But why? And what was it her father had said? Something about an old enemy. But how could anyone have known they were there? None of it made any sense.

'But, as I said, I'll be happy to take you.'

'I couldn't think of it. You've done so much already. I'll always be grateful to you. I mean, I could have died, surely, if no one had found me.'

'I don't think that was intended. He would have made a better job of it. To be blunt.'

'You're right.' The half-hearted way her hands had been tied. 'Anyway, I'm incredibly lucky that you were passing. And now here you are, driving me around when you must have been going somewhere yourself.'

'Nowhere important. It doesn't matter.'

'Of course it does. You're just being polite.'

'Okay, a boring and unnecessary meeting. I'll hardly even be missed. I was taking a detour, hoping to arrive late. They'll all be droning on for hours with nothing settled. Somebody can easily sum up the whole thing for me in a couple of sentences.'

She smiled. 'All right, then.' She could have asked him what he did, she supposed; but it was none of her business, and after today, she would never see him again.

And it seemed odd to be talking about office meetings when, in one day, her life had been turned upside down. But it wasn't going to stay that way. She would regain control of all this and sort things out. Once she had seen Dad and heard the doctor's verdict.

If he had to stop in for another night or so, she would try to book the cottage for longer; or, better still, get a B&B nearer the hospital. Phone work and explain. Calming, having to think of all these possible arrangements. Taking her mind off her ordeal and what she might find at the hospital.

But what she did find was the last thing she could have expected.

# 4

They pulled up at the entrance Jess had left the night before. There was nowhere to park.

Jess said, 'It's okay. I'm fine now. But thank you so much for everything.'

'No way.' He shook his head. 'I'll quickly dump the car somewhere and come back. To make sure you're okay. And maybe you should give your face a bit of a wash? Or you'll be giving your father a fright.'

'Should I? Well, yes. I'm sure you're right.' She glanced down at herself.

'The rest of you isn't too bad, considering.'

'Okay, then. You can wait here for me.' Maybe that sounded a bit grudging after all he'd done. 'I'm going to ask at Reception and find out which ward he's on. My dad's name is Leo Dryden. And okay, you can follow me up.'

He must have parked the car nearby — and very probably illegally — because he was coming back in as she left the Ladies and approached the desk. He'd been right, her face had been covered in smudges of dust. The hospital staff wouldn't be too keen on someone looking like that entering a sterile environment. And he had been totally right to consider her dad's reaction.

'My father was brought in last night? I don't know his ward number.'

The receptionist consulted a screen, frowning. She murmured a number, almost to herself.

'Thank you very much,' Jess called back over her shoulder. Refreshed by the brief wash, she was full of determination now. In no mood to be hanging about. She set off down the corridor, looking for direction signs, her companion following.

He said helpfully, 'She seemed to be trying to tell you something else.'

'Oh, probably that I'm outside visiting hours. But I'm sure they'll let me see him for a minute or two, just to make sure he's okay. And I need him to give me directions for where the car is.' She flashed him a strained smile. 'I can be very charming when I try.'

'I'm sure you can.'

They were both scanning the various signs and arrows as they walked. No discussion, no argument. She was pleased to see that, like her, he was good at making swift decisions. A good companion to have in a crisis.

Here they were. She walked in briskly and approached the nursing station, turning quickly to scan the faces in the nearby beds. 'Excuse me.' She smiled, softening her voice. 'I know I'm way too early, but my father was brought in last night? A suspected heart attack. If I could just see him for a minute or two, please?'

The nurse frowned. 'I'm sorry, but — '

'The thing is, we came here in an ambulance, and I need to ask him where he left our car.' She leaned forward. 'And I desperately need to know how he is.'

'I'm very sorry, but your father discharged himself early this morning.'

'What?' Everything stopped. That couldn't be right. 'But — he was ill.'

'Against our advice, obviously.' The nurse softened a little. 'He didn't actually seek any advice. Dressed and left, with all his belongings.'

'He only had the clothes he arrived in. But — where is he? Where's he gone? Why hasn't he phoned me?'

'I'm afraid I have no idea. But when you find him, could I stress that you should tell him in the strongest possible terms to seek medical help as soon as he can?'

Jess knew her shock must be all too evident. She was actually clinging to the desk for support. Behind her, she felt a strong hand holding her arm. She said, 'Of course. His phone will be out of charge. He does that all the time. Totally hopeless.'

The nurse leaned closer. 'Look, I

shouldn't be telling you this, but we hadn't found anything in the tests. When the doctor came round later this morning, he would probably have been discharged anyway.'

Her companion said, 'Thank you. Thank you very much. You've been most helpful. And I'm so sorry you've been messed about like this.' He could obviously turn on the charm too.

'Don't worry,' the nurse was saying. 'I expect he will have made his own way home by now.'

They left the ward, Jess still feeling dazed. A wave of anger swept over her. What on earth did he think he was doing? And where *was* he? She muttered, 'You idiot, Dad.'

'This way. You mentioned a holiday cottage? And that you have the address?'

Jess took a deep breath, trying to calm down. 'You're right. If I'd known, we could have gone straight there. I'm sorry to mess you about. My dad can be such a pain sometimes.'

'Aren't they all? And my name's Oliver, by the way.'

'Jess.'

'So, let's see the address you have. And don't start telling me I've done enough. For my own peace of mind, I need to deliver you to a place of safety.'

Jess raised her eyebrows, trying to make light of that. 'Sounds very dramatic.'

'The way we met was dramatic.'

She nodded. 'Yes. Okay, then. Thank you. Again.'

They made their way to the back street where Oliver had parked. 'No ticket,' he said cheerfully.

For the first few minutes, as he began driving out of the city, neither of them spoke. Jess was thinking furiously. What was happening? Why had he discharged himself? Had he not thought how upset she would be?

But then, he would have assumed she'd spent the night at the cottage; and that if he set off early enough, he would get there before she left. So what must he be thinking now? And why had he not tried to ring her? He could have charged his phone once he got to the cottage. If he'd thought of it. If he'd brought his charger.

Oliver said, 'Have you any idea who could have done that to you?'

'Pardon? Oh, no.' Obviously Oliver's thoughts had moved on. 'I don't know. He didn't take anything. My purse and phone were still in my bag. And why go off and leave me?'

'Perhaps someone disturbed him?'

'Out there? A passing dog walker, maybe. Or a farmer. But why leave without his car — and how?'

'It wasn't too far from the main road. He could have got someone to pick him up. Or hitched. A jealous ex seeking revenge?'

She almost laughed. 'I doubt it. My exes all left amicably.'

'No enemies?'

'Of course not.' She stopped, again remembering that odd remark of her father's. But why kidnap her? What would be the point? She shivered.

'You've remembered something.'

'No, I don't think so. Put it down to stress.' Perhaps, when she'd found her father and retrieved the car, they should phone the police. Would it be too late to do that now? Would the fake taxi be where they had left it? Perhaps she should have thought of all that before. But she had been so desperate to get back to her father.

Something occurred to her. Why hadn't Oliver suggested ringing the police? He had seemed so concerned and ready to help, but wouldn't most people have been dialling 999 straight away?

She opened her mouth to suggest it. Or at least to ask why he hadn't. And stopped. That worrying remark of her father's was bouncing around in her head again. Would the police be a good idea? No, not until she had made Dad tell her what he'd meant. Then they could decide whether to involve the police. Oliver could tell them where he'd found the taxi because she hadn't a clue.

She must have glanced at Oliver as she was thinking all this. He nodded at the satnav. 'Okay? We're just about there. Should be somewhere along here.'

'Yes.' Her voice was high with relief. 'That little track off to the left. That's it.' At last, for the first time in hours, she had ended up where she was supposed to be. And soon she would find Dad, and everything would be sorted out — when she had given him a good piece of her mind.

The small, single-storey, sprawling cottage with the cramped windows seemed so welcoming as she ran along the uneven path with Oliver following.

'Dad?' Jessica stopped. The door was locked. It couldn't be. She knocked, bruising her knuckles. 'Dad, it's me. Jess.'

Oliver said quietly, 'You don't have a key?'

'There's only one. My father had it.'

She frowned. 'But when we arrived, he knew where to find it.' She went round the side of the cottage and found the inverted plant pot by the old pump. 'Yes, it's here.'

'Rural security. Problem solved.' There was an unusual note in Oliver's voice.

Jess snatched up the key and rushed past him to unlock the door. 'Dad?' Stupid — with the door locked and the key in her hand, there was no chance of her father being inside.

The cottage was small. One bedroom — hers — and a folding bed-settee in the kitchen diner and living room where her father had slept. The rooms seemed empty now. When they'd left the previous morning, her father's bag had been in one corner, a blue jumper strewn over a chair. She glanced into the bathroom. Only the bottles and jars she'd brought with her. Nothing of his.

Hopelessly, she opened the bedroom door. No reason for anything of his to be in here.

'What's that?' Oliver said sharply, behind her.

'Where?' On the pillow, there was an envelope addressed to her. At last. Relief and hope surged within her. This would explain everything. He hadn't left her adrift after all. She tore it open and stared at the single sheet of paper.

*Sorry, Jess. I had to leave early.*
*Oliver will drive you home. You can trust him. See you soon. Keep safe. Love x.*

Oliver's voice was calm. 'What does it say?'

She turned, staring at him. Filled with a cold anger. 'I'm surprised you need to ask. Here.' She thrust it at him. Considering the strength of her fury and hurt at her father's betrayal, her voice seemed wonderfully steady.

He read it, several times. 'This tells us nothing.'

'Wrong, Oliver. It tells me a great deal. You already know my father. You knew him all along. And didn't think to mention it.'

He didn't even seem apologetic. 'I expected to find him here. I was told he would explain everything to both of us. I've been let down too.'

She began to pace up and down, as if she was on the phone. 'Just passing? That's what you said. No way. You knew I was in that car boot. You knew exactly where to find me. In fact, I'll bet my father told you where I'd be. You both betrayed me. The two of you together. How could you do that?'

She stopped pacing, walked up to him, and peered closely into his face. He stared back, not flinching. 'In fact, I never got a good look at the taxi driver's face. He had a cap pulled down. That could have been you.'

'No.' Oliver was angry now. 'I wouldn't have done that to you. I only knew where to find you.'

She nodded, reluctantly. 'Okay. Your voice isn't the same. And I should have realised there was something not quite right. The whole set-up wasn't vicious enough. I had enough air, I could breathe. Getting my wrists untied was easy.'

'But it doesn't excuse it.'

'Too right, it doesn't. Well, then, there's one person I do want to see soon as — or sooner than that, even. I'm going to have it out with him, I'll tell you. So I'd better go along with this, I suppose, and let you take me back home, to Leeds.' She gave a hard laugh. 'If I can believe any of it. Anything he says. Or you say. Just tell me, Oliver, before we set off, what are you to my father? And why should I trust you?'

He said, without even blinking, 'I'm your brother.'

# 5

Jess said nothing, staring at him. At last she said, 'I don't have a brother.'

He shrugged. 'I'm afraid you do.'

'My dad never — ' She stopped. Obviously there was a lot her father had never told her. Why not this too? 'Oh, whatever. Just now, I trust him less than I trust you. So let's go.'

They were both silent, getting back in the car, fastening their belts. Packing had taken Jess less than five minutes. She'd hardly had the time to spread herself around in the cottage.

She glanced back at it. *How lovely,* she'd said when they arrived. *Well done, Dad. A brilliant find.* Feeling exhilarated and happy with everything, because at last — at long last — he was going to tell her about her mother and how she had died. *Yes,* he'd said, solemnly, *it's time you knew. I owe you that. And her. I'll show you her grave and tell you about her.*

But that hadn't happened. An opportunity wasted. And she didn't even know whether she could find the grave again. But she wasn't leaving without another look. She said suddenly, 'My mother's buried in a churchyard near here. I want to see it again.'

'What?'

'Do you know where it is?' She gave another of those harsh laughs she hardly recognised in herself. 'Sorry. I was forgetting. She must be your mother too.' She paused. 'Or are you a half-brother?'

'No. I'm a full brother. But, Jessica — ' He stopped. 'Our mother is still alive. As far as I know. Unless something's happened? Something I don't know about?'

Jess felt dizzy. As if she wasn't really there. What was going on? 'No, no. Dad said she died years ago. Not long after I was born.'

'I'm afraid he was lying.'

'Yes.' There was no point in denying it. She was turning possibilities around in her mind. Why had he done it? Presumably their mother had left him — and this was his embittered reaction. Unless he'd made some kind of mistake . . .

She said slowly, 'I suppose he must have been devastated when she left. Perhaps it was the only way he could cope with it.'

'That could be one way of putting it.'

Jess gave him a suspicious, sideways glance. He had chosen those words too carefully. He knew more than he was telling her.

Right. Begin at the beginning. Ask the right questions. 'So, if you're my brother, where have you been all this time? Ah — if you're so certain our mother's alive — were you with *her*?' That would make sense.

He said, 'No. I was not.' He was staring straight ahead, at the road.

'And your name?'

'Not Dryden. Not officially.'

'Were you adopted?'

'You could put it like that.'

'But why? Why couldn't you stay with us? Or our mother? Look, I'm sorry if this is painful for you, but I need to know.'

'Of course you do. And there are a lot of things I need to know, too. And the arrangement was that Leo Dryden, our father, would tell us everything today. Both of us together, when I brought you back to this cottage.'

'Having *rescued* me.' Her voice was sarcastic.

He shrugged.

'Well, you know more than I do. So can we start with that, please? And then, when we find Dad, we'll both be at the same starting point.' She straightened her back. Now she was getting somewhere. 'So — you knew where to find me.'

'Yes.'

'Who told you?' Jess had an uneasy feeling that she already knew the answer.

'Leo Dryden. Your father.' He gave a swift grimace. 'Our father.'

Did he have to answer so briefly? She felt like shaking the information out of him. 'Why? Why would he do that? And don't try to pretend you don't know. You don't just agree to rescue a girl from a car boot — a girl who happens to be your sister — without wanting to know the reason.'

'He was protecting you. Apparently.'

'What? A very odd way of going about it. And who from? Surely you didn't believe that, did you? Stop shrugging your shoulders like that. It's very annoying.' She was drumming her fingers on the car door. 'It seems to me the whole thing was engineered to avoid telling me about my mother. His supposed heart attack was very convenient.'

Oliver laughed, for the first time with what seemed to be genuine humour. 'I don't know why you're bothering to ask. You seem to be doing a great job working it all out for yourself.'

She nodded. Yes. Shut up, Jess. If she

happened to be wrong on any of this, he only needed to agree with her theories and she would never get anywhere. 'So tell me.'

He paused. 'As you said. He didn't want to tell you about your mother.'

She was still thinking. 'There's more to it than that. I can see he might engineer the illness — but what about the rest of it? Why did he tell me he was worried about me?'

'When did he say that?' Oliver's tone was guarded.

'In the hospital. One of the last things he said.' She frowned, remembering. 'That he was worried about me, and there was an old business partner looking for him. Obviously someone he'd fallen out with. So where do you come into it?'

'I was adopted. When I was very small, by a business partner of his.'

Jess said quickly, 'Presumably the one he mentioned. Who is he?' She stopped. 'Was Dad right to warn me? Is he dangerous?'

'I would say he could be, when crossed.'

Jess took a long, slow breath. 'At least you know who he is and what he looks like. You'd better give me a nudge if he shows up.' She hoped she sounded calmer than she felt. But surely, if he had adopted Oliver, he couldn't have been that bad? She said cautiously, 'Were you okay? Did you have a happy childhood?'

He shrugged. Again. 'Happiness is relative, isn't it? You accept what there is, not knowing any better. I don't suppose I was that unhappy. You could say I suffered little physical harm.' He stopped. 'But I was never loved.'

'Oh.' Her childhood had involved moving around a lot. More than anyone else at the different schools she attended. Her dad would come home and say, 'Guess what? We're off again.' She had accepted it. New jobs, promotions, area offices, transfers. She considered this, frowning. Had she ever had a sense that they were hiding from someone or something? Or running away?

No, Dad had always seemed laid-back

and casual about it, every time. But he'd always been expert at sliding away from difficult questions and changing the subject. She had never thought anything of it. If her friends' fathers were watching football on TV, they weren't too good at answering questions either.

Oliver tensed. She realised that he had been looking in the mirror far too much for at least the last five minutes. Without warning, he crossed a lane and shot off up a slip road into some services.

Jess jerked forwards in her seatbelt, clutching onto the door handle. 'What's the matter?'

'Nothing. Everything's fine.'

'Yeah, sure.' He wasn't even pulling into the car park but was off again, taking the service exit road. Jess turned, expecting to see another car in pursuit. The narrow lane was empty. 'Who are we running from? Did you think someone was following us? Was it this person Dad warned me about?'

'Could be.'

She wasn't at all certain whether she believed him. He could have put on a show of being pursued, to try and convince her. 'Not funny, switching lanes like that for no reason. You could have killed us.'

'I didn't, though, did I? Listen, Jess, a bit of erratic driving is the least of our worries, believe me.'

Jess grunted, not convinced. She remembered her father's note. *You can trust him*. But could she? And why should she, when it was all too obvious that she couldn't trust her father?

When they got back to Leeds, she would be wanting some answers.

\*  \*  \*

When they reached Leeds, however, there were more answers needed than Jess could have ever anticipated. She said, 'Ignore the satnav at this junction. You need to turn left.'

'Yes, I know.'

Jess raised her eyebrows. But of

course he knew. Why be surprised? If he was in close contact with her father, he would probably have his address as well as his mobile number. No doubt he had known *her* address all along, too. She hunched her shoulders, not sure she liked the idea of that.

He said, 'Do you live with your father?'

'What?' She was feeling so edgy now that she was unable to take the question at face value. Did he really not know? Or was he trying to deceive her? He seemed to know everything else about her.

She paused. 'No, I moved out last year. But I'm round here a lot.'

He nodded. 'With your washing?'

She laughed. 'Excuse me? No, certainly not. I might do his sometimes if he's got behind with it. Mostly, he's okay with looking after himself. Very self-sufficient.'

'Yes, I get that impression.' Another of those remarks made in that level tone, giving nothing away and yet concealing an inner bite.

Jess fingered her phone. Dad must be assuming they would be on their way by now, but maybe she should text him to let him know? No. Keep him guessing. If he knew where she was, he might run off again. The more she thought about that, the more likely it seemed. In fact, he would probably want to keep her in the dark, too; she was certain his phone would be turned off.

They were almost there. What would they find? Yet another note, wardrobes empty, all the suitcases gone? *Sorry, Jess, have had to rush off to Spain suddenly*. Or France. Or Germany. And none of it true. She took a deep breath. She had to face it: he had let her down badly. She might well find it hard to forgive him.

No more speculating; they were here now.

The car doors slammed almost in unison as they got out. Jess wanted to leap out and run in. She forced herself to slow down. Be cool and deliberate.

He said, 'Are you okay?' There seemed to be genuine concern in his voice.

Jess felt the onset of angry tears and gritted her teeth, fighting them. 'Fine, thanks.'

'I can wait here if you like.'

'No. Come with me.' She managed some kind of a grin. 'You deserve answers too.'

'Too right.' He looked up and down the road. 'I don't see the car.'

'We usually park round the back.' The handle gave beneath her hand, and the door opened. Yes. He was here. She turned to grin, properly, at Oliver. 'It's okay.' She took a couple of steps into the hall and stopped. No, it was not okay.

The tiny workstation under the stairs had every drawer open. Contents strewn across the floor. All the doors out of the hall wide open.

Oliver, close behind her now, gently moved her aside and strode past her. 'Wait here.'

'No way.' And what was he expecting to find? The house was silent, the intruders long gone . . . surely? She swallowed. What Oliver was expecting was all too obvious. But she had no intention of hiding from it. If something bad had happened to her father, she wanted to know. And see it for herself.

She pressed into the front room, almost pushing Oliver out of the way. Not caring about the mess in there, not yet, only that the room was empty. Back room. Kitchen. All the same.

Oliver was striding up the stairs and Jess followed. Both bedrooms, bathroom. All empty. She swayed for a moment with relief, clutching the banister rail.

'He's not here,' Oliver said.

No. So where was he? She said, 'It's not just a random mess, is it? They were looking for something.'

'Yes. Systematic. And it looks like they didn't find it.'

'Oh? Oh, I see. They've gone through every room. But where's Dad? Have they taken him instead? Or is he hiding somewhere?' She took out her phone.

Oliver said, 'Worth a try.'

Before she could do anything, it rang. The jangling ringtone, that had seemed so witty and personal, now only made her jump.

'Hello? Dad, is that you? Where are you? Are you okay?'

'I'm fine. Don't worry.' His voice was so loud that Oliver could hear it clearly. Jess held it away from her ear.

'But Dad, someone's wrecked the house.'

'No need to worry about that, Jessica. I will clear it up when I get back. I am just phoning to tell you that everything is fine, however it looks.' Suddenly, he lowered his voice and spoke rapidly. Jess could hardly hear him. 'Listen, you need to go to your flat and find an envelope with your name on it. It's inside that cookbook I gave you last Christmas.'

'But I use that all the time. There's nothing in there.'

'There is now.' She winced as his

voice boomed out again. 'Go back to your flat and stay there until I ring again. Oliver will look after you. Trust him. Did you get that, Jessica? Go back and stay there. Until I ring again. In about two hours' time.'

A confusion of sounds now, as if someone else had said something. Maybe more than one person. A sharp noise as if he'd dropped the phone. Nothing more.

She looked up at Oliver as the blood drained from her face. 'Did you hear all that? I think someone's holding him somewhere.'

'Sounds like it. What was that bit in the middle? Something about cooking?'

'I have to find an envelope in a book.' She paused, trying to think. Her hands were shaking — but there was no time for that. *Pull yourself together, Jess.* 'That's what he really wants me to do. Go back to my flat and get this envelope.'

'And then get the hell out of there,' Oliver said quietly.

'Yes, that's what I think too. He never calls me Jessica. I think he was repeating what he'd been told to say.'

'So in two hours — someone will come looking for you.'

'And I won't be there. Not sitting there waiting for Dad to call me.' She took a breath. 'Okay, let's go.'

They said little during the short drive to the city centre. Jess was trying to process her new feelings. From being furiously angry with her father for what had happened in Leicester, now she was fearful. What must he be going through? What had *they*, whoever they were, done to him? When he'd been trying to sound unlike his normal self, obviously to warn her, had there been an added weakness in his voice?

The car swung off City Road and paused at the gate to the car park beneath the flats. She said, 'Sorry, wasn't thinking. Here's my key card.'

The gate was already whining and opening. 'No need. I have one.'

'What? How?'

'I live here too. Even have my own parking space.'

'Well, you would.' She knew there was suspicion in her tone. 'Isn't that a bit of a coincidence?'

'Not really. Depends how you look at it. Presumably your father had a lot to do with buying yours? Same with me. Said he had a contact with the owners and could get a good deal.'

'Why?'

'To compensate for giving me away as a kid. That's what he said.'

'But not what you think.'

He nodded. 'You're sharp. Maybe it was to keep an eye on me. To ensure he knew where I was.'

'Not to get *you* to keep an eye on *me*? To spy on me?' She was ready to be angry again.

'All depends how you look at things. A more positive take on it might be to enable me to watch out for you.'

'I don't need watching out for.'

'Are you sure? Because I think we both do.' He nodded as he swung into his space. 'You're bristling again, Jess. You do it all the time. I'm sure you do a great job of looking out for yourself, in general. But somebody is out there who may well be interested in us and for all the wrong reasons. The people who have your father. Our father. And I don't know about you, but I would prefer to avoid them for now. At least until we know more about what they want.'

'Right.' She followed him to the lifts. 'Makes sense, I suppose.'

He stood back from the buttons. 'Your call. Your address.'

'Mm.' She pressed the control panel, thinking hard. What did he mean, *more* about what they wanted? She didn't know anything about what they wanted. A slip of the tongue meaning nothing? Or did it mean that Oliver *did* know something?

But first things first. Maybe this mystery envelope would explain, at last.

Everything was just the same in the communal areas. Grey carpeted corridor, a row of white-painted doors. A window by the stairs looking out onto the inner courtyard, with the terracotta blocks of the neighbouring flats and other buildings overlooking the cars below; the car park crossed by the wooden pedestrian bridge leading to the main communal entrance to her block.

It seemed weeks ago now since she had left, instead of little more than a day. She took a breath before inserting her key. What would she see here? More chaos?

Nothing had changed. She said, 'No one's been in. I know, I don't pack tidily. Things get flung about a bit. But not the books.' She was already striding over to the shelves.

Oliver said, 'Nice wall.'

'What? Oh, the collage of Leeds scenes. Yes.' Where was it? After everything that had happened, she wouldn't have been surprised if the book had been missing.

'My flat has one too. Same position, black and white collage almost identical. The views are slightly different.'

'Yes, my dad found an Art student to do them, I think. Turned out quite well.

Here's the book.' She flipped through the pages; and, yes, the envelope was there too. Almost too easy.

Her fingers would hardly obey her as she tried to rip it open. It seemed unexpectedly firm. Only one item inside — and not a piece of paper. She slid it out, forgetting to breathe.

It was a photograph of a girl, about her own age. Walking along a street, dressed for winter in a blue coat and knitted hat and scarf.

She stared at it. Turned it over before looking inside the envelope again. When Oliver spoke, she almost jumped. She'd forgotten he was there. He said, 'Who is that?'

She paused, breathing hard to contain her disappointment. 'I have absolutely no idea.'

# 6

Sam woke with a cloud of confusing images in her head. Nat's sudden appearance; the look on his face. How she had been left standing alone in shock after his abrupt exit. How she had become aware of how cold she was. Turning, as if in a dream, as she heard someone call her name.

Lucas had been there behind her with her coat in his hands. 'What are you doing out here? Are you all right?' His voice was gentle, concerned.

'I felt a bit hot. It came over me suddenly. I thought I'd splash some water on my face and then I saw the open door — and I needed to be out in the fresh air.'

He said only, 'But you're all right now? Come and sit down.' Gently placing her coat round her shoulders and leading her back. 'Here's your bag.

You left that too.'

'Yes,' she said meekly. She had got away with it. Lucas seemed to have accepted her feeble explanation, and she was grateful — so very thankful — for that. She resisted the temptation to look back. Nat would get in touch with her. He had almost agreed to that, hadn't he?

Lucas said, 'Come and have a coffee and get warm.' He wasn't hassling her. For several long minutes he allowed her to sit quietly as she tried to make sense of things — and failed.

The waiter brought the coffee. It was hot. She sipped, beginning to relax.

Lucas' voice was level and unhurried. 'So, who was that?'

'Oh, no one. I made a mistake.' She said the first thing that came into her head. 'I thought it was someone I knew. But it wasn't.' She added into the silence: 'He was very nice about it.'

Lucas nodded. 'I'm sure it happens all the time.'

She closed her eyes briefly. Did he believe her?

Lucas had walked her back to her block of flats, across the wooden walkway, and left her at the entrance. He had said he would be in touch to make sure she was okay. Sam had never known him to be so considerate.

This morning, thinking about all that — although still shying away from the pain of Nat's rejection — she wondered if the way Lucas had reacted had been a bit odd. Had he believed her too readily? And why? That wasn't like him. Or had he not pursued the questioning because he knew the answers already? Had he seen Nat? Had he got close enough?

She sat upright abruptly. That look on Nat's face. Had Nat seen *him*? She had wondered, yesterday, whether Lucas had been the object of her mother's warning.

No, of course not. She breathed deeply and slowly, calming herself. If she had been in danger from Lucas, no way would Nat have left her there with him. Whatever had gone on to make him feel he had to disappear from her life, it couldn't involve Lucas.

So, what to do next? Stay here in her little flat, where she knew she was safe? She could phone in sick; her head was throbbing, so it was almost true. She could wait for her mother to ring and ask her what was going on. Hopefully she would be able to go in to work this afternoon. Yes, that seemed the best option. *Try to relax*, she told herself firmly.

She padded into the kitchen, made herself a cup of coffee and sat on the sofa, looking at the black and white collage of views of Leeds that covered one wall of the small sitting room. She had loved this feature from the start. Looking at it was always calming as she recognised one view or another. Recognising more every time she looked. Some of the locations were beginning to seem very familiar now. There was the square she had run across last night. *No, don't think about that. Look at something else.*

Wait a minute. Something was different. She was looking at a photo of a girl walking over a bridge — head down against the wind — in a woollen hat and scarf.

Sam felt ice cold, from the back of her neck right down her spine. She was seeing a photograph of herself. Crossing the walkway to the flats. And that picture hadn't been there before. She was sure she would have noticed.

Every thought in her head was stilled. There was only one thing screaming out at her. Someone had been in here and stuck it on. Since yesterday morning? Although, she had hurried off to work as usual without hanging around. It could have been during the day when she was out. But there was no sign of a break-in — or was there? She stood up. *Check it out. Check everything.* Her chest froze. Supposing they were still here somewhere?

Unlikely, because the flat was tiny; but all the same, she crept round it with her heart thudding. Bedroom, bathroom, kitchen and living room, and the built-in cupboard in the hallway. It took only a few minutes to know the flat was indeed empty and there was no one under the bed or behind the curtains, which were the only places you could possibly hide.

And no sign of any forced entry. She ran her fingers along the door surround of the patio doors opening onto the wraparound balcony.

A few moments of blessed relief before the fear flooded back. Someone must have a key. That meant they could come in any time they chose. She was no longer secure here, in her little refuge. Undoubtedly, she never had been.

There was only one course to take. She had to get out. Run away. Go somewhere else. She grabbed her clothes and locked herself in the bathroom to shower and dress. Where could she go? Work must be safe, surely?

And then what? Go and stay with somebody? She hardly knew anyone here. Claire? Lucas? No, not Lucas.

Not when she didn't know whether she could trust him. Perhaps it had been him anyway? He knew where she lived. He didn't like to give up when he'd decided on a course of action.

No, calm down. Now she was being over the top when all she needed was a locksmith. Yes, that was it. And Claire was always keen to help with anything, so she would be sure to know someone who could do the work. Although maybe she should get the landlord's permission first? Obviously you couldn't just change the locks without telling them.

She would have to ring them, whoever they were. She had done everything through some agency or other she'd forgotten the name of for the minute. Must find the paperwork and get hold of them. And if she couldn't find the number, she could pop out to their office; it wasn't far. Would they understand the need for urgency? Of course they would. If they had a lot of properties to handle, this kind of thing must happen all the time.

Or, not exactly this kind of thing. Ordinary breaking and entering must happen. She thought, *I wish*. How simple would that be? You would just phone the police, be given a crime number, look at your insurance policy —

Because if she did ring the police, what would they say to her? It was doubtful whether coming in and leaving a photo stuck to a wall was any kind of crime at all.

Okay, never mind all that. She would get the locksmith first, and worry about the landlord afterwards. Take control. Phone Claire.

# 7

Jess glanced at Oliver, eyes wide. Yes, he seemed puzzled; but not, she thought, anything like as devastated as she was. She swallowed and found her voice. 'Does she mean anything to you? Do you recognise her?'

He said slowly, 'No.'

'I thought we would get more than this. A message, an explanation.'

'Y-e-e-e-s. That would have been good. But obviously we're expected to sit here like idiots and wait for a call. To tell us what to do next.'

'Yes. Two hours, he said.' Jess looked at her watch. 'Presumably from when he spoke to me. That means we have just over one hour left now, if that.'

Oliver said, 'They may be nearby already. Watching us.'

'Yes, that's all too obvious. We need to go.'

Oliver was looking out of the large window. 'I can just about see my flat from here.'

'Great. Good for you. Will that be any safer than mine?'

'Doubt it. No, I was checking out how we might be able to keep watch ourselves.' He took out his phone.

'What are you doing?' Jess knew her voice was rising and didn't care. 'We need to get out of here ASAP, and you're making phone calls?'

He was half smiling. 'It's okay.'

Jess didn't intend to waste time, whatever he felt like doing. She was darting into the bedroom. When would it be safe to come back here? Her backpack was already packed for the ill-fated weekend in Leicestershire. She had all the essentials. Maybe a good idea to add a couple of things.

She pushed in a framed photograph of her father. Might be useful if he was missing. Had a sudden thought and exchanged her coat for one warmer, cleaner, and a different colour.

Oliver appeared at the bedroom door. 'Ready?'

'If you are.' She knew she sounded sarcastic.

'I've booked a room at the hotel.' He gestured towards the window. 'Straight across, with a good view.'

'Ah. I get it.' She grinned. 'Sorry.' They would have a clear view of anyone seeking to access the flat on foot via the bridge and the central doorway. Although not if they came up in the lift from the car park. 'How will we be able to see if anyone comes in?'

'We'll leave all the lights on.'

Jess went for the lamps and the wall switches, keeping well back from the windows as she did so. 'That should do it. Though if anyone's watching already, we may have given ourselves away.'

'A risk we'll have to take.'

She nodded and followed him. Locked the door with a cold feeling across her shoulders. When would she be able to come back?

Oliver said, 'We can go down through

the car park and then split up. I'll meet you in the hotel foyer.'

The flats took up two sides of the large, asymmetrical open courtyard; the rear of the hotel took up another, with its frontage onto the major road into the city centre. The last was a glass-sided block of offices. Jess walked quickly, keeping her eyes ahead.

*Look natural.* If she looked over her shoulders, she would draw attention to herself; and if she did spot someone watching her or following, what good would it do? What action could she take? But not turning back took every effort of will. Once out on the main road and with other people about, she felt better.

She walked into the hotel foyer — confidently, she hoped. Oliver was already there, looking at a newspaper. 'Hi, there!' He smiled at her and his face lit up.

She blinked for a moment. He had only just left her, hadn't he? No, stupid. They had to look as if they were meeting here and were pleased to see each other. 'Hi to you too.' Smiling back.

'I've checked in and got the keys.'

'That's fine.'

It was exactly as Oliver had said. The twin room overlooked the central square and had a front-row view of her flat. Strange to look into it from over here. The lights illuminated it well, just as they had hoped. It was clearly empty and as they had left it.

Oliver took the single chair and positioned it a few feet away from the window. Although it was unlikely that they would be seen through the tinted glass. Jess knelt on the floor. She still had a good view. If anyone moved out there, you noticed straight away.

She said, without taking her eyes from the courtyard, 'We have plenty of time now. For you to tell me everything else you know.'

He didn't turn his head either. 'What I know?'

'No use pretending. You know a great deal more than you've told me. If we're to get to the bottom of all this, we need to share our knowledge.'

His voice sounded neutral. 'I agree. Seems fairly obvious that good old Dad isn't giving anything away easily. Just leading us on some mad treasure hunt. More of a time-wasting exercise than anything else, I suspect.'

'Wasting time until what?'

'Exactly. But I'd rather we found out for ourselves than just let it happen.'

'Let's stick to what we know, please. You knew I was in the boot of that car and where to find me. We've established that — and that my father told you about it. How long have you been in contact with him?' She thought, *And without anyone bothering to tell me.*

'I met him last week. For the first time in — twenty-five years, it would be. And realised for the first time that my good deal on the flat had been his doing.'

'Met him by chance?'

'No. I'd been searching for him for a while.'

'Oh, since you were eighteen? And

were entitled to look?'

'It wasn't a formal adoption. But my adoptive parents never made any secret of it. Whenever I asked a question, it was answered. But not in the way you might expect. No kindness, no pretence of my being *special* or *chosen*. I was told I'd been 'surplus to requirements', and it had been in my father's best interests to pass me over to them.'

'That sounds incredibly cold — and cruel, even.'

'Yes, it was. Franklin, my adoptive father, took me to score a point, not because he wanted me. His wife, my new mother, was more approachable, I suppose. But she always said, whenever they argued or if I misbehaved, that she hadn't been consulted. That I hadn't been *her* choice.'

Jess was shaking her head. 'That's dreadful.'

'Anyway, you want to know about *your* father. Finding him wasn't too difficult, with the help of the internet. Even though he'd moved several times.

And then, when I was so close that I had all his contact details to hand, and was only considering how best to approach him and what I needed to say — he came to me.'

Jess frowned. 'It doesn't sound as if he was hiding from *you*, then.'

'No, he wasn't. Not by then. But my vague ideas of recrimination and holding him to account, making him realise how hurt I'd been — all that got knocked aside.'

'How? What did he tell you?' Yes, she knew her father could put on the charm when he wanted, but surely even he would find it difficult to override all that hurt.

'By what he wanted me to do.'

'Go on.'

'This is where you come in. Eventually he told me about you. And that you were in danger. And where to find you: in the boot of an abandoned car in Leicestershire, as you know.'

Jess stared at him, trying to make the facts fit.

He gave a laugh. 'I received the final information through a third party. I can't say I was too keen on the idea. I half-thought I was being stitched up. That as soon as I reached the car, I'd be surrounded by the police. But then again, I couldn't take the risk of leaving you there. So I decided it wouldn't hurt to take a cautious look.'

'Wait a minute. How long after he approached you did he tell you all this?'

He half turned to look at her, still watching the courtyard access, his face expressionless. 'Not long. The final message came through the night before. Early evening, about seven. Even the time I should leave was specified. I left early the next morning while it was still dark.'

'But I was okay the night before. I was with Dad in the hospital at seven in the evening. None of it had happened.'

'I'd worked that out.'

Her fears were confirmed. 'My father knew *everything* in advance. Why? Why would he do that to me?' She felt like howling with anger. She was only surprised that she sounded so calm.

'To save you from something worse, maybe?'

'Oh.' Jess was silent for a while. Oliver said nothing. She said, 'You mean, the people who have him now? But it doesn't make sense. Surely he could have arranged something less horrible? He must have known how terrified I would be. Why couldn't he just tell me?'

Oliver raised his eyebrows. 'And you would have listened? And done what he wanted? Without asking questions and making objections?'

No, of course she wouldn't have. *But*, she argued silently, *there were all kinds of alternatives he could have arranged instead.* Like what? If the stakes were so high and he had to be certain that she would be kept out of harm's way . . .

'But I can't see that it's worked. I don't feel safe now, with my flat under siege.'

'We're not doing too badly. We're one step ahead.'

'I'd rather be several hundred steps ahead, thanks. And we don't even know who they are. But they know who we are.'

Oliver said nothing.

'Or do you know who they are?'

Oliver was suddenly tense, leaning forwards. 'There, look. That girl.'

Jess had allowed her watch on the bridge to lapse. She jerked her head to look where he was pointing. Yes! There was no doubt. She recognised the hat and scarf. At the end of the bridge, the girl stopped to answer her phone, her face clearly visible.

'It's the girl in the photograph.' She leapt up. 'We should follow her.'

'No. Too late. We couldn't catch up with her to see where she goes inside. More sense in waiting for her to come out again.'

Jess sighed in frustration; but he was right, of course. 'She must live here too.'

'I've seen her before.' There was a different note in Oliver's voice. He was suddenly more alert. 'And I remember where. I knew there was something familiar about that photo. She's our sister.'

# 8

Jess had a wild feeling that she had new relatives coming at her from every direction.

'What? I didn't know I had a sister. Are you sure?'

'Yes. Almost one hundred percent certain. I can remember what happened, just. The last time I saw her — and you — I would have been about four.'

Jess tried to sound brisk. 'You have the advantage there, then. I can't remember a thing. I've no idea what you're talking about.'

'You wouldn't. You were only about two, I would say. And our sister was even younger.'

She couldn't decide whether to believe him or not. But he seemed expert at drip-feeding information, controlling exactly how much she knew and when. No doubt there was some purpose to that, but she was beginning to find it irritating.

'You can't stop there. You'd better tell me exactly how much you remember and what happened.'

'To me?'

'To all of us, obviously.'

'You're right. We need to work together. And we'd better make sure we keep in contact. We'll exchange mobile numbers.'

'Okay.' She paused. 'You're not thinking of running out on me, are you?' Smiling to show she was only half-serious. Except that she was. Her father had told her to trust him, but she wouldn't put anything past him. Or the two of them. For a start, he couldn't possibly recognise that girl now from seeing her when she was two.

He grinned; warily, she thought. 'No way. As I said, we have to work together.'

'Too right.' Replacing her phone in her pocket, she said firmly, 'And now tell me what you know.'

Across the courtyard, the lights in her flat went out.

Jess had almost forgotten why they were there, lulled by the inactivity behind her windows and distracted by Oliver's bombshell. She gave a gasp of triumph. 'Got them! Did you see anything?'

'Only a brief movement by the kitchen.' He swore softly. If he was putting it on, he was making a good job of it. He sounded genuinely annoyed. 'We didn't even see them come in. I've slipped up. They'll go down to the car park when they leave and we won't see them. We've wasted our chance.'

'And what are they doing?' Jess pressed her face to the glass which didn't help. 'What do they want?' She was feeling sick at the outrage of it. That was her space. How dare they, whoever they were?

'Can't tell. Look, you have my number. I'll go and watch them come out from inside and you stay here. If they go down to the car park, I can follow them. Whoever sees them first can inform the other.'

'Okay.' There was hardly time to do anything but go along with his suggestion. Only when he had rushed out did objections to Oliver's plan surface. He'd taken the best chance of catching them for himself, but she had a car in the car park too. And why split up at all? She wasn't convinced that she would see the intruders from here.

Had Oliver made a genuine mistake in his reasoning? Or was all this part of some bigger plan? But she'd had every chance to spot the flaw in his logic and had missed it.

Would she even be able to tell, from here, when the door onto the corridor opened as the intruders left? And how could Oliver watch her door from the corridor without the intruders seeing him as they came out? There was nowhere to hide. The stairs in the corner maybe — but if they chose the lift, they would go the other way. He would be just as likely to lose them.

He should have known that, if he lived here too. He'd made the suggestion and she had agreed with it too quickly. No time to do anything else.

Nothing she could do about that now. She sat, staring out, convincing herself she could see occasional movement behind the glass. Although they seemed to be taking care to keep away from the windows. But then, there was only the sofa there. If they were searching for something, they would be rifling through drawers and cupboards.

Or were they searching? Perhaps they were waiting for her to return, to walk into their trap. If so, they would be there for a while. Would they give up when she didn't appear? And if not, Oliver would be observing the front door for a very long time.

They *were* moving about in there. What were they looking for? She didn't have anything useful.

Her phone rang. She snatched it up. 'Yes?'

'They're leaving. Get to the car park

as fast as you can and you can come with me.'

'Right.' Jess frowned. Had they had enough time to get that far? But now the lights in the flat were switched on again. They had covered their tracks and she could see it was empty.

Below her, a figure came through the glass doors and was walking across the bridge. 'Oliver? Wait. I can see that girl again. Do as we said. You follow them and I'll follow her.'

'No, Jess — '

She cut him off. If he waited for her in the car park, he would lose the intruders anyway. It was obvious. What was he thinking of?

Jess had acted on impulse, and wasn't sure what she was going to do when she caught up with the girl. Except that she must not let her get away. Not without finding something out about her. Jess had no way of knowing when she would see her again.

Without further thought, Jess was running down the hotel stairs and out onto the street. Yes, the girl had taken the paved walkway leading to the city centre. She was still in sight, and Jess was about to catch up with her and get some answers.

Or was she? Jess slowed as they passed Bridgewater Place. What *was* she going to say? She could hardly launch into the unlikely-sounding tale so abruptly. *Hi, I think you're my sister.* Think about it. Oliver hadn't mentioned the relationship straight off. And even when he had, she hadn't been totally convinced. She was still unsure about it. But there hadn't been time to think properly. No doubt Oliver had been counting on that.

So for now, Jess would keep the girl in view, sister or not, and see where she went. If she was going to work, that could be useful information; they could find her there whenever they liked.

The girl was moving briskly after they passed under the railway. Jess did the same. The pavement was not crowded, but there were enough people moving in the same direction for Jess to avoid being noticed. Even if her quarry stopped and turned round — and she was giving no sign of that.

As they approached the Headrow and crossed to the central reservation dividing the carriageways, Jess hung back a little. She was closer to the girl than she would have liked as the crowd herded together in the middle. Waiting to cross as the traffic swept past.

Next to her, an arm lunged forwards, striking the other girl squarely in the centre of her spine. She began to fall forwards as Jess, her instincts reacting more swiftly than her thoughts, caught hold of her shoulder and pulled her back.

There was a screeching of brakes. Someone screamed briefly. Jess turned, because next to her, another figure was turning also, running back the other way to the pavement they had left. She caught a glimpse of a dark coat, mid-length glossy brown hair. Jess remembered seeing her without noticing her. She had been walking alongside Jess, as if following the other girl too. The girl who was now shaking and half-sobbing in Jess's arms.

'It's all right,' Jess said. 'No harm done. You're okay?'

The driver in front of them swore through his window and accelerated away. Fortunately, the car behind had stopped without hitting him. That driver gave them a rueful wave and a shrug.

'Yes,' the girl said.

'Come on, you need to sit down.'

'I'll be fine in a minute. Just a bit of a shock.'

'Yes. It would be.' No need to wonder, in the event, how to get into conversation with her.

Jess led the girl across the Art Gallery square and they perched on the first of the long, wide steps. 'Better take it easy for a bit. What happened?' For the first time, Jess had a good view of her face. Gentle blue eyes and fair curling hair. She didn't seem to look much like Leo Dryden, or Jess. Or even Oliver. But that would have been too easy. And family resemblances were often more subtle than that.

The girl was taking deep, panting breaths. 'You'll think this is stupid, but I thought someone pushed me. I'm sure they didn't. That wouldn't make sense. Would it?'

'No.' Jess shook her head.

The girl turned to look closely into her face. 'If they had, you would have seen them, wouldn't you? And thank you so much, by the way.' She smiled. 'I think you probably saved my life.'

'Oh, more than likely.' Jess tried to laugh it off. 'We were all so squashed together. Some of the people behind us should never have set off when there wasn't room in the middle.'

'Yes, that would be it.'

'Would you like a coffee? I'll buy you one. A hot drink would do you good.'

'It should be me treating you. To thank you.' The girl turned to look up at the white stone frontage of the Art Gallery. 'I'm supposed to be meeting someone for lunch. Please come too.'

She paused. 'If you're not doing something else?'

'I'm not. I'll be happy to.' No need to worry about encouraging the girl to talk as they mounted the steps. She was hardly pausing to finish her sentences. But that was probably the euphoria of her near miss. Jess said 'Is the small café downstairs okay, if there's room? Or would you prefer the Tiled Gallery? Oh, you said you were meeting someone, didn't you?'

'That's right. I haven't been to either yet. We were meeting in the Tiled one.'

When they were sitting down with their drinks, Jess broke into the torrent of words again. 'Thanks for the coffee. And my name's Jess Dryden.' She smiled encouragingly.

'Sam Turner. Sorry, I don't usually talk this much.'

'I expect it's the shock. It can do funny things. Do you work in Leeds, then? Or are you shopping?'

Yes, Sam worked in Leeds; and yes, she was happy to tell Jess the name of the firm and the street it was on, and how she had been transferred from London and hadn't been here long.

Brilliant. Almost too easy. And one of Leo's business interests, too. No surprise there, Jess supposed. 'Actually, I think I've seen you before? Going into the flats off City Road?'

Sam's face lit up. 'Yes, I live there. Don't say you do too?'

Of course she did. They would be best friends in a matter of minutes. Except that Jess wasn't too sure now how to introduce the possibility of their closer relationship. She wished she could have made Oliver tell her more before she'd rushed off. And it wasn't that simple, was it? How safe was Sam now? She could leave as Sam's friend arrived, knowing she could easily catch up with her anytime she liked. But the person who had pushed her was still out there.

*No, come on, Jess. Get real.* She was getting paranoid now, seeing conspiracies everywhere. Obviously this was engendered by her own fears, based on her own situation. She had caught the merest glimpse of that other girl and reacted automatically. They had been all crowded together, as she had told Sam. The other girl might have been trying to attract Sam's attention for some reason. Or been shoved herself as others pushed on to the island. Or it could have been a mugging attempt. And then the perpetrator had run off, horrified at what had *almost* happened — and accidentally.

For Sam to have been in any danger, she would have had to have been deliberately targeted.

Her phone rang. Jess glanced at the number that came up and made a show of pulling a face. 'Sorry. I'd better take this.'

'That's okay.'

She nodded her thanks. 'Yes?' She stood up, walked away to the doorway where the stairs to the library began. Mouthed to Sam, 'Work.'

Oliver said, 'You'll have to get back

over here.' His voice sounded strained. 'Have just had a call from your — our — father. If we don't do something quickly, they're going to kill him.'

# 9

Sam turned, hearing Claire's voice behind her. 'Sorry I'm late. I don't know where the time went, somehow.'

'Never mind, you're here now. But you've missed all the excitement.' Sam was still feeling cold and remote inside, but telling Claire, she managed to turn the accident into a humorous incident. Blaming herself for teetering on the edge of the traffic. 'But the girl behind me pulled me back, just in time. That was so lucky. I've asked her to join us. Her name's Jess. You don't mind, do you? She seems really nice — and guess what, she lives near me.'

'That's great,' Claire said. 'You need to make more friends.'

'She's just on the phone at the moment.' Sam turned and stopped. Jess was walking back towards them, her face white.

Sam half-rose. 'Whatever's the matter? Has something happened?'

Jess seemed to be trying to laugh and not managing it too well. 'Nothing to worry about. But I'll have to go and see to it.'

'Of course. Perhaps we can meet up another time?'

'Certainly can. I'll give you my number.'

After exchanging numbers, Sam glanced after Jess as she hurried off. 'What a shame. It would have been nice if you could have met her, properly.'

'Never mind. Another time. As you said.' There was a strange note in Claire's voice.

Perhaps she was jealous, Sam thought doubtfully. After all, she had been very kind in taking Sam under her wing.

Claire was looking down at her fingers. 'The thing is — I'm just wondering. That girl, Jess, was behind you, wasn't she?'

'Yes.'

'So, how do you know *she* wasn't the one who pushed you?'

Sam stared at her. 'What? But that doesn't make sense. She saved me. Like I told you.'

'She said she did. But you couldn't see her, could you? She could have pushed you and then caught you.'

Sam sat back, making a dismissive gesture with one hand as if swatting the ludicrous idea away. 'Why would she do that?'

'I was thinking about it.' Claire leaned forwards. 'She might have wanted to get round you, to get to know you. Because after what you thought she'd done for you, of course you were grateful. Only too happy to come for a coffee, swap phone numbers, make friends with her.'

Sam grinned. 'Why would she bother? I'd have been happy to do that anyway. Making friends in a new place isn't all that easy.'

Claire looked offended. 'You've got me. And if you don't mind my saying, you've kept yourself back a bit. You keep saying you want to be on your own.'

'I know. I'm sorry.' Sam paused. She

couldn't possibly tell Claire that she had felt an instant connection with Jess, which had overridden her cautious reticence. Claire would feel more sidelined than ever. 'There's been so much to do,' she said, knowing how feeble that sounded. 'Look, if I've seemed standoffish or anything, I'm sorry.'

Claire stared at her before, to Sam's relief, breaking into a smile. 'Yes, of course. Ignore me. It was just the shock of hearing what had happened, making me touchy. If you'd been hurt, I could never have forgiven myself. I'm sure this — Jess, is it? I'm sure she's fine. Just as you thought. Meet up with her by all means.'

Sam managed not to raise her eyebrows. 'Thanks,' she said solemnly. 'I probably will.'

'I could come too,' Claire said brightly.

'Well, yes, I suppose you could.' Was Claire organising her again? No doubt she meant well, but Sam wished she wouldn't.

Claire was saying, 'I wonder why she

had to rush off so suddenly? That seemed odd, didn't it?'

Sam shrugged. She had been wondering that herself, but with concern rather than curiosity. Whatever it was, she hoped Jess would manage to sort it out. She had looked so stricken. She said, 'Go and get some food if you like.'

'Oh, have you had yours?'

'I'm not hungry.' Sam shook her head.

Claire stood up. 'That will be the shock kicking in. Don't worry. I'll sort something out.'

'There's no need. Honestly.' Too late. Claire had bustled off. Sam leaned back in her chair, putting a hand over her eyes. Her phone beeped and she reached for it. Immediately she was alert, weariness gone.

*Meet me in the café by the lake in Roundhay Park 3pm. Xxx*

It had to be Nat. She didn't recognise the phone, but he must have a new one now. And he always signed off with kisses like that. It was their own private signal. She replied rapidly, her hand fumbling in her eagerness. *Will do. Sam Xxx*

She had so much to tell him. She realised just how much she wanted to pour everything out to someone she could trust. The worry about her mother, the strange photo in the flat — and now the near-accident.

Claire was back. 'Not much of a queue, so that was lucky. I've got sandwiches to share. You have to eat something.' She put the plates down on the table. 'Am I sounding bossy? Sorry. No pressure. No problem if you still don't want anything.'

'That's fine. Thanks. I do feel hungry now.'

'I knew you would. Particularly when you're having such a worrying day. Did you get sorted out with the locksmith? Forgot to ask when I rang to ask you out to lunch. And why did you need one? You didn't have time to say.' Claire was leaning forward again in that avid way she had.

Sam thought quickly. 'Yes, thank you so much. He was brilliant. He came round straight away. It's all sorted now, thanks. It wasn't anything really.' She paused. Somehow she didn't want Claire exclaiming and speculating about the strange photo. 'Just that I'd lost my spare key and didn't want to risk somebody finding it.' How pathetic that sounded. She said brightly, 'Better safe than sorry.'

'Oh, I see.' Claire sounded disappointed. 'I thought you must have had a break-in at least.'

'Nothing like that. All fine.'

'Good. And you've polished off those sandwiches. Well done. Do you want a piece of the chocolate fudge cake? Very scrummy.'

'I don't think I can manage that, thanks.' Sam knew she was hopeless at lying, and how tangled she became if she tried. She really couldn't keep this up for long. 'I know I've managed to eat the sandwiches, but I'm still feeling shaky. In fact, I'm starting to feel really tired now. I don't think I can come back to work after all. But I'm sure I'll feel better tomorrow. Can you tell them for me, please?'

'Oh, dear. Poor you. Of course I will. I'm sure you're doing the right thing. And take tomorrow off too, if necessary. I'll explain for you.'

'Goodness, no. I'll be fine by then.'

Claire frowned, hardly listening. 'I don't think you'd better walk back to your flat. How far is it exactly?'

'I'll get a taxi. Don't worry.'

'Good idea. Shall I come with you? To make sure you're okay?'

'Definitely not.'

But she couldn't prevent Claire from organising the taxi for her and supporting her arm as they walked outside. Helping her in, nodding attentively so that Sam had to give the driver her address. Waving as at last they were setting off along the Headrow, leaving Claire safely behind, Sam said, 'Sorry to be a nuisance, but would you mind if we go to Roundhay Park instead?'

Not a problem. And the driver was

able to drop her off at a car park very close to the café she needed. She would be early, but that didn't matter. And even with the locks changed, she hadn't wanted to go back to the flat. Not yet.

She went inside, ordered a latte, and chose a table by one of the windows overlooking the lake. She had a good view of the only entrance — but wished she could see more of the paths, approaching from several directions. She tried to sit still, wanting to be turning her head every way at once. Knowing she mustn't. She would only draw attention to herself, and that was the last thing Nat would want. And there was still plenty of time. It was only a quarter to.

A shadow fell across her. Just when she had been looking out at the lake and hadn't seen him coming. She looked up gladly as someone slid into the seat across the table. Her smile froze. Lucas.

She stared at him with horror. What was he doing here? Nat would see him and avoid her. The meeting she had so looked forward to was ruined. Worse, Nat might think she had broken her word to him and told Lucas about him.

Lucas smiled. 'Hello, Sam.'

'I'm sorry. I'm busy. This seat's taken. I'm waiting for someone.' She knew how impolite that sounded, but she couldn't help it. She had to get him to go away.

'I know. You're waiting for me.'

The realisation sank in slowly. She hadn't recognised the phone number. She had assumed it was Nat. But the signal with the kisses? She said, 'The message wasn't from your phone.'

'I have more than one.'

'Oh.' Sam looked down at her hands, misery threatening to overwhelm her. No. She would not let him play with her like this. He had planned it. He knew all too well what he was doing. And the kisses? Maybe she had left her phone on the table when she'd rushed out last night.

She looked up, meeting his eyes

directly. He looked mildly surprised but interested. Another attempt at putting her off.

'This has got to stop, Lucas. I told you, I want the freedom to meet new people and make new friends. I don't want to have you following me around all the time.'

'So, which new friend did you think was texting you?'

'That's no business of yours. I mean it. I've asked you to give me space and you still persist in turning up.'

He shrugged. 'Consider it done. Of course.'

Sam stood up. 'I'm leaving now. And you are not to follow me.'

'Fair enough.' As she began to walk away, he said quietly but calmly, 'You're making a mistake. Nathan Grant isn't what you think he is.'

She stopped. A voice in her head was screaming, *Keep going. Don't listen.* Her feet turned as if of their own accord. She had to know. She sat down again. 'I don't know what you mean.'

'I think you do. Or you would be out of that door by now, ignoring me.'

'You'd better explain yourself.' She thought, *He can't.* He was bluffing. He must be.

'You came here hoping to find him. And I think you've found him already.' He leaned forwards, clasping his hands, resting them on the table. 'What has Nathan told you about me? And why were you so ready to believe him? Is that fair when you haven't heard my side of it?' He laughed. 'No wonder you didn't want to get back together with me.'

Sam frowned. She hadn't the least idea what he was talking about, but would he believe her if she told him so? Probably not. He would believe what he had decided to believe, knowing Lucas. She would get further by pretending to go along with him.

'Why should I believe anything you say?' she said cautiously.

'Because I may have been a selfish arrogant prat when we were together, but I've never lied to you.'

'If you say so.'

'I do. None of this is what you think. I only want to protect you.' He paused. 'I'm in law enforcement now.'

The last thing Sam had expected him to say. 'You're a policeman?' Already she was thinking, *What a strange way of putting it, if so.* Law enforcement. If he was with the police, why not say so?

'No, not exactly. I'm on the side of the law. But on a freelance basis.'

A kind of private detective? Bounty hunter? Was he even doing this — whatever it was — legally? 'How do you mean?'

He laughed. 'You've never had any idea how expressive your face is. That's what I've always loved about you. I always know what you're thinking.'

'Not necessarily.' Sam tried to keep her face wooden. 'And we'll keep off the mechanics of our past relationship, if you don't mind. I asked you a question.'

'Well — I'm in the protection game.

I'm involved with security. Not a process many people are aware of. Not the way I manage it.'

Sam sighed. 'Are you actually going to get round to telling me what you protect?'

'In general, anything that might be targeted. Art collections, expensive jewellery. I'm often employed by some very rich people with a lot to lose.'

'As a high-power security guard.'

'No, strictly background. I keep my ear to the ground and discover the threats. And that's my point. Nathan Grant is involved in some very dubious stuff. Dangerous to himself, and also to anyone who hangs around with him. He's best avoided, trust me.'

'That's just it. I don't. I can't. You have to prove it to me.'

He was shaking his head. 'Can't do that. My work is ultra-confidential. I shouldn't even have told you this much.'

'I see.' She was becoming annoyed. 'Can you give me any idea of what you're protecting currently? Without jeopardising confidentiality, of course.'

'Yes. I'm protecting you.'

'Me? Whatever do you mean? From what? And who's employing you? No, you're making this up. Unless — is it my mother?' And if what he had said was true, how could Mum possibly afford him? Was he doing it for nothing?

'No, no. And I wouldn't take your mum's money anyhow. Okay, I wasn't supposed to tell you any of this. I was just to keep a watch from a distance.'

'Hanging around outside the office? Trying to get me to go out with you again?'

'That would have made it easier. But I've realised that's a no-go, don't worry. But since I can't be any closer to you, I have to warn you. You're putting yourself in danger by trusting the wrong people. And Nathan Grant in particular.'

'I know what it is. You're jealous of him. But too bad, I love Nat.' She glared at him.

'I know you do. He's a lovable guy — and he's been very clever. Look, you're angry. Of course you are. As I said, I don't expect you to love me again. None of this is about that. Just be very wary of him. Besides — ' He sat back in his chair, nodding seriously. ' — from what I saw, he doesn't want you around anyway. Why not go with that and think yourself lucky?'

That was true. Her throat was tight and she wanted to cry. She gritted her teeth. There might be some truth in what Lucas was telling her. She *had* thought that Nat was going to say, *It's not safe.* But she no longer wanted to confide in Lucas as she'd intended. The more he strove to earn her trust, the less she trusted him.

She said, 'Maybe. Thanks.'

'I know I've messed up with you, big-time. I was a fool and look where it's got me. But truth will win out in the end. I can wait.' He stood up. 'If Nat should come sniffing round, just remember what I've said, and keep out of all the dark stuff he's involved in. And I'll give you the space you asked for. I won't contact you again until you contact me.' He rested both hands on the table and leaned forwards towards her. She found that she was staring back at him as if mesmerised.

He said, 'If you need help — anywhere, anytime — I'll come. Don't hesitate.' Lightly, he brushed her hair with his lips. And was gone.

# 10

Jess saw Oliver waiting on the corner of Park House Drive and the Headrow, looking up and down the street, his face relaxing into relief when he saw her. She called, 'What's happened? Why is he in danger?'

These pavements, backed with tall grey offices and financial buildings, were much less busy than the shopping streets. There was no one near enough to hear — but he made a point of waiting until she reached him before replying. 'He can tell you himself. Come on.' He took her hand.

'Where are we going? Is it far?' And, as he pulled her through a side entrance leading to a doorway she would hardly have noticed, 'Is this safe?' The door was featureless, no visible lock or handles, presumably opening from the inside to give vehicle access to the loading area at the back.

'We're fine.'

Yes, they must be, here in the middle of the city, only yards from the main thoroughfares. And if her father had asked for her, she must go. No question. There was a narrower door further along, and abruptly they were through it and inside, descending a flight of stone stairs.

Jess was getting a mix of warning messages now, overlaid with the need to see her father after all this chasing around and false trails. Yet another door at the bottom. A corridor. She was losing her sense of direction. Were they under the rear yard or beneath the street now? They were moving through a labyrinth of passageways and cellars.

Oliver stopped. Someone was standing outside another door. His whole stance, legs slightly apart, hands clasped, told her that this man was on guard — but more of a doorman than military. Oliver seemed to know him. 'Okay?'

'Go on.' The man answered without looking at Jess. As if he had been briefed to show no interest in her.

Oliver opened the door. Jess said, 'Wait!' This felt so wrong. She should have asked more questions when they were outside. Too late now. She was already into the small cellar, where daylight came through the single half-window at ceiling level. And rising from the only chair, arms outstretched, was her father.

He had never been a demonstrative parent, but without thinking about it, Jess flew into his arms and buried her face in his shoulder. Feeling an urge to cry. *Help me, Dad. Look after me. I can't deal with this.* She lifted her head. What was she thinking of? *Don't be stupid.* Crying just wasn't an option. She had too many questions. Even more now than she'd had this morning.

'This is like a prison, Dad.' One chair, even a basic narrow bed against one wall.

He smiled and shrugged. 'Only temporary. We have something someone else wants, that's all.'

She stared at him, narrowing her eyes. 'Nobody stopped me coming in to see you. Can you leave if you want to?'

He gave a balancing gesture with one hand. A gesture he used a lot when he had no intention of telling you anything. Was this horrible little cellar a hideout and protection — or enforced? As usual, he would only tell her when he was ready. Unless he could be persuaded to let something slip.

'What is this thing they want? What can I do?'

'That's it, exactly. We need you — and your sister.'

Hearing him coming straight out with it, without any denial or prevarication, was a shock. Jess had thought he would be reluctant to admit what Oliver had told her. 'My sister?'

'We won't waste time. I know Oliver has told you about her already — and about himself. I'm sorry, Jess. For everything — that I had to hide Oliver and Samantha's existence from you and from each other. It was a terrible thing to do. But I had no alternative.' He bowed his head.

It was happening again, as it always did, in the face of her father's immense charm. She couldn't help wanting to reassure him. But was the bowed head a true expression of regret — or done to prevent her seeing his eyes? *And don't kid yourself, Jess, he's quite capable of lying while looking you straight in the face.*

She said, 'I'm sure — ' She swallowed and began again. 'I'm sure you did what you thought was best. At the time. But Dad, I need to *know*.'

'Yes. You do. And I will tell you, I promise. But for now, we have to deal with this situation.' He gestured to the cellar walls. 'I wish I could have handled things differently, but for now, I have to do what I'm told. And to achieve that, we need the three of you together.'

'Why? That doesn't make any sense.' She knew it was pointless. She sighed. 'Okay. You want me to find Sam.'

'And bring her here. Yes.' He nodded, smiling. As always, he was so sure she would do as he asked. He was like that with everyone.

'Look, Dad, it's not that simple. How do I know she'll be safe if she comes here? Or that any of us will be? You said these people are dangerous. What's likely to happen next?'

Very softly, looking directly into her eyes now, 'You will just have to trust me, Jess.'

But that was the problem. 'Dad, I might risk it for myself. I can't ask it of *her*.' She had only met Sam briefly but she seemed so sweet and vulnerable and trusting. No doubt Sam would agree to help like a shot.

'I'm sorry. You have to. This is serious.' He smiled, his face relaxing disarmingly. 'It's not like you to be so cautious. Where's my headstrong Jess who rushes into everything without stopping to think?'

Yes, where was she? Jess felt a dozen years older than the girl who had stood

136

in the cemetery. 'Too much has happened. I spent last night locked in the boot of a car; I can't go back to my flat because I've seen it being entered and presumably searched for something or other; I seem to have a brother and sister I'd never heard of. And I can't tell whether you are a victim of all this too.' She hesitated. 'Or not.'

'I'll tell you. Very soon. You have my promise. But I need to tell all three of you together.' He paused. 'I owe that to Sam, at least. I've let you down, all three of you.'

Jess felt herself wavering. Why did he always have to sound so plausible? No, there were too many unanswered questions, and yet again, he was sliding out of it without telling her anything. She needed to know.

She said, slowly and deliberately and using the direct stare technique herself, 'I'll trust you. I'll bring her. But only if you first answer one question, just one.' The question that had made everything kick off. 'How did my mother die?' Her heart was thudding. She could feel sweat on her palms.

He shook his head, a hand to his forehead. An act to gain sympathy? She was seeing him through new eyes. She had always known he was doing it, but she had laughed about it in the past. Too handsome for his own good. She would say, 'Stop posing, Dad, I'm so not impressed.'

Now however, his voice was cracking with what seemed to be genuine regret. 'I'm so sorry, Jess. I thought I was doing it for the best. The best thing for you. I only wanted to save you pain.'

'What is it?' She felt like screaming in frustration. 'Tell me.'

'Your mother isn't dead.'

Jess nodded. 'At last. You've admitted it. Why did you pretend for all those years? You put me through so much misery and loneliness. I've missed so much.'

'No. You and I were happy together. You know we were.'

'So many lies. You never had a heart

attack. More pretence. I thought, last night, locked up on my own, that you might have killed her. Or had her killed.' Anger was taking over now. 'So where is she? Where has she been all this time?'

'I wanted to protect you. She left us. And I don't *know* where she's been all these years. Not for want of looking, either. I've been trying to find her, all along.'

'And Sam?'

'Yes, your sister will be able to fill in the gaps. Your mother took Sam with her.'

'Splitting the family apart,' Jess said bitterly. 'That's terrible. But why?'

'I wish I knew more. I couldn't believe it at the time. But bring your sister here, as we agreed, and she will be able to answer all your questions about your mother. Maybe Sam knows why your mother chose to leave us so suddenly. And chose to conceal the two of them so cleverly.' He shook his head sadly. 'To go to that extent, to escape us. Not caring about the hurt she was causing. But enough of that.' His voice was suddenly brisk. 'Bring Sam here, and we can sort everything out. I promise.'

Another promise. But what else could she do? There were scraps of disguised truth in his account. It was identifying them that was difficult.

She sighed. 'Okay.'

'Your brother will go with you.'

'Right.' She looked round at Oliver belatedly, wishing she had been able to watch his face during her father's list of excuses. But Oliver had been standing behind her. Now he was nodding. Encouragement? Reassurance? Difficult to tell. And how much did he know? Had *he* been telling her the truth? Not the whole of it, she suspected. Things were moving too fast — and, at the same time, not fast enough. But for now, she would have to go with it. This was all she had.

Her father said, 'You have her number, don't you? Ring her.'

'Now?'

'Yes.'

Jess hesitated. She would rather have done this alone, but couldn't think of a convincing reason. Besides, with the security guard or whoever he was in the corridor, where could she go? She took out her phone.

'Sam?'

'Yes?' Sam sounded hesitant. Upset, even. 'Oh, Jess.' Her voice brightened. 'Hello. Are you okay? I've been so worried about you since you had to dash off like that. Was it bad news?'

'I know. I'm sorry. Are *you* okay?'

'Well, yes. It's just — something somebody said to me. I'll be fine.'

'That's good. Look, I — need to talk to you. I can't really do it over the phone.' Her father was shaking his head, frowning. Jess ignored him. 'Where are you now?'

'I'm in a big park. Roundhay, is it?'

'That's right. I'll come and meet you, shall I? And I can explain about why I had to rush off. Are you somewhere you can wait, without getting too cold?'

'Oh, yes. I'm in a café by the lake. I don't need to go anywhere.'

'Perfect. I won't be long. See you soon.'

Her father said again, 'Oliver will go with you.'

'There's no need. I think it will be better if I go on my own. Less threatening.'

Her father laughed. 'You're not going to seem threatening. You're telling her something wonderful. But Oliver can hang back a bit if you think that best.'

'No, I still think — '

'He has his car parked here. It will be much quicker — and for coming back. Don't forget, I'm not making my own decisions while I'm in here. It's difficult.'

Oh, yes. These dangerous people there didn't seem to be any sign of. Jess looked at Oliver. Perhaps he wouldn't get in the way too much. He shrugged, his face noncommittal. An expression he seemed to be good at.

Once again, Jess was sure there was more going on than her father was revealing. Was this just one of his games, or something more sinister? She gave in. 'Fine. Let's do it.'

# 11

A welcome distraction, Sam thought, to have someone else to worry about. She was filled with relief at first, just to hear Jess's voice. Jess had looked so shocked when she'd had to rush off. Something was obviously very wrong.

But Sam's relief soon melted into other concerns. She had hardly known Jess any time at all — and had liked her straight away. And now she could tell from Jess's voice that something was still affecting her. She wasn't imagining it, even though Jess had seemed a strong and resourceful person.

So of course she'd agreed to wait until Jess could turn up here. No reason not to. Sam just hoped it would be something she could help with. After all, Jess had saved her life. Or saved her from a very nasty accident.

Strange, how she had related to Jess

straightaway; whereas Claire, who had been very kind and had made a point of taking Sam under her wing — well, Sam didn't feel able to welcome that wing as she should. No doubt she was being uncharitable when Claire meant well.

She heard footsteps behind her. Jess? She turned.

Nat was sitting down where Lucas had sat only a few minutes ago. 'Sorry I'm late.'

'But I don't understand.' Sam looked at her phone. '*You* arranged to meet me here?'

'Of course.' He grinned. 'Who were you expecting?'

'You. Of course I was.' She frowned. 'But then someone else came and said he'd sent the text.' She added, 'But he's gone now.' And leaving a nasty cloud of doubt behind him.

'Sounds confusing. Anyone I need to worry about?'

Sam said slowly, 'I don't know. Oh, not in that way. I don't care about him. Not at all.'

'Let's forget about him, then.'

'Yes.' She hesitated. She should ask Nat about what Lucas had said about him. She must. And then Nat could deny the allegations and dismiss them, and everything would be all right. But Jess would be arriving soon.

'Is everything okay?'

'I'd almost forgotten. I'm sorry, I'd given you up. I'm meeting someone else in a few minutes. She seemed so upset and shocked. I just wanted to help.'

'That's what I've always loved about you, Sam.'

'I don't know what I can do. She said she wanted to talk to me.' Sam stopped. What if Jess's crisis was personal in some way? She wouldn't be expecting Nat.

He said, 'Whatever her problem is, maybe I can help too.'

'Thanks,' she said awkwardly. Some instinct made her glance up. Too late. Jess was standing in the doorway with a dark man who seemed familiar. Sam frowned.

Nat said lightly, 'She seems to have brought reinforcements.'

Sam nodded. 'Yes. Maybe he's part of the problem?' He seemed to be muttering something to Jess, one hand on her arm as they stood there. Perhaps asking her if he should stand back?

Sam waved, half-standing. Jess turned to her friend and nodded. They both came over. Sam turned to Nat and caught a strange expression on his face. Wariness? Even enmity?

Sam felt as if someone should ease the awkwardness with a beaming smile, a cheery 'Isn't this nice?'. Her mum was good at that kind of thing — or could be, when she wasn't being edgy herself.

'This is Oliver,' Jess said.

'And this is Nat.'

There were nods of greeting between the two men. Sam was certain that they knew each other already. How weird. But, whatever; this wasn't about these two. She said, 'Are you okay, Jess? I was really worried about you.'

'I'm okay, yes. I'm just — worried

about someone else.'

'Yes? Is it something I can help with?'

'Well, yes, it is. The thing is — and I know this will come as a shock — but you're my sister.'

'I see.' Sam heard her own voice, sounding completely calm. She nodded, aware that a huge, foolish smile was spreading across her face. 'I've always wanted a sister, that's brilliant. Amazing. And I'm so glad it's you. This lunchtime, I felt like I'd known you for ages . . . ' She stopped. Jess was only marginally reflecting her happiness. 'But something's wrong?'

'Yes. It's my dad. Our father. I don't quite know how to explain this, because I don't understand it myself. But he's got himself into something — I don't know what it is. Something — '

'Illegal?' Sam said helpfully. 'Dangerous?'

'Maybe. He says he needs to tell us both together.'

Nat said quietly, 'Would you rather I left?'

Before Jess could answer, Sam said, 'No. Please stay.' She stopped, suddenly remembering what Lucas had told her about Nat. Oh, no. She should be questioning Nat independently, seeking verification — or at least a reaction, so she could decide for herself who she believed. But his face was giving nothing away. He was leaning back in his chair as if completely relaxed, his face showing merely a polite interest.

She knew him too well because she loved him. He was faking it. Her heart sank. She turned to Jess again. 'Okay,' she said slowly. 'Where is he?' Because there was no option but to find out. This was someone she'd always wondered about and pictured, although her mum would never talk about him. And, yes, that meant her mother was Jess's mum too — and Jess had grown up without her.

Jess was saying, 'He's in Leeds. It's a bit odd; he's staying in the cellars under some offices. But I'm not sure whether that's because it's a good place to hide, or whether he's being kept there. By someone he won't tell me about — or not yet. He'll tell us together.'

'I see.' Sam nodded. She was surprised at how calm and rational she felt. Perhaps she was still in shock.

'We've been able to come and go,' Jess said. 'Nobody stopped us.' She sounded as if she was convincing herself. 'We've only been once, but it was fine.'

'Good. That's good.' Sam knew she was nodding too much. She made herself stop. 'We? Us? Who do you mean?' She looked from Jess to this Oliver; she felt he'd been looking almost suspicious, or as if he'd been assessing her.

Now he said, 'Yes. I'm your brother. There are three of us. Pleased to meet you.'

They shook hands solemnly over the coffee cups. Sam thought, *No wonder he seemed familiar. That must explain it. Mustn't it?*

She said, 'Only three?'

He laughed. 'Afraid so. And I was brought up separately too.'

'Oh! By another relative?'

'No.' The word sounded a little too definite.

Jess said quickly, 'By a — family friend, as far as I can make out. Dad's going to explain the whole thing to us. And also explain how we three can be instrumental in getting him out of the hole he's in.'

Sam was nodding in agreement again. Of course she would help, whatever it took.

Oliver said, 'Don't jump in and agree. We don't know what it is. Don't commit yourself to anything — and particularly not to him.'

Sam looked at him. Something was wrong. This went far beyond all the lovely tearful reunions you saw on the TV programmes, which she was always glued to whenever they were on. Had even imagined how she would feel, being presented to a father and a whole new family. But she had pictured him marrying again, having left her mum. And that she would be the eldest.

She said, 'Yes, you're right.' She smiled at Jess to soften the words. 'We'd better find out what it is first. But what happens now? Can we go today?'

Oliver and Jess looked at each other. Jess said, 'Yes. Better had. Presumably when this is all sorted, it will be safe for me to go back to my flat.'

Oliver said, 'You can come to mine if you want.'

'How do you know that's okay? Have you checked it lately?'

'No.' Oliver turned to Sam. 'We both live in the same block as you.'

'Oh! Really? What a coincidence.' Sam frowned, wondering if she had seen him around. Or Jess.

'No. A coincidence is one thing it's not,' Oliver said. Jess was texting, frowning at her phone.

Sam said, 'But I found the flat myself.' She shook her head. No time for that now. She would have to consider it later sometime. Though maybe Oliver was right. She remembered the photo of herself on the wall and shuddered. She turned to Nat, saying impulsively, 'Are you coming too?'

'I don't think so, thanks. This is obviously a family thing and I haven't been invited.'

Again there was that tension between Oliver and Nat. Sam could feel it without looking. The way their eyes flickered away from each other.

She said, 'I'm inviting you.'

'I think,' Nat said, 'that I can be more helpful in keeping out of it. I'm not sure this is a safe suggestion, not for you. And someone needs to know where you've gone.'

'You're right to be cautious,' Oliver said suddenly. 'But I'm willing to guarantee the girls' safety. Nothing will happen to them.'

Jess rolled her eyes. 'You both know more than you're saying. I'm getting fed up with this. Well, I'm certainly going — if only to find out what's going on. Unless one of you is going to tell me? Now?'

Nobody said anything.

She shook her head. 'I thought as much. I'm sick of all these hints and snippets of info. I'm going.'

Sam said, 'So am I.' She wanted to meet her father. Had to, whatever he was mixed up in.

Oliver smiled. 'That's good. So that's settled.'

And Sam suddenly remembered where she had seen him before. Last night in the restaurant — with Lucas.

# 12

Jess was still thinking as they drove. Neither of them had answered her spoken challenge. Far too simple. And where did this Nat fit into things? Sam had seemed so very happy to see him — but surprised, too. And Nat? Did he feel the same way about her? Jess wasn't sure.

And something else, pushed into the back of her mind to consider later. That man leaving the café as they approached. It had been Lucas, who worked for her father. She had known straightaway, with an electric spark of recognition.

Only as they were turning through the featureless door did she say, 'Can't we park somewhere else? This seems too enclosed.'

'Where then?' Oliver said. 'Down by the railway? Too far.'

Already the steel door was closing

behind them. Jess said suddenly, 'And what's with this *I'll guarantee their safety* thing? How can you say that?'

'Because I will.' He was concentrating on parking in a tight space — or pretending to.

'*How* though? Specifically?'

He looked straight at her. 'It will all be okay. Trust me.'

She sniffed. 'But do I?'

He shrugged. 'Nearly there.'

Inside, nothing had changed. They trooped down the stairs. Sam had said nothing in the car, and she was still silent; but as she walked next to Jess, her arms were held tightly at her sides. As if she were protectively closing in on herself. *What on earth is she making of all this?* Jess thought. *And if Oliver is proved wrong, I'm responsible for getting Sam into it. Whatever it is.*

The guard, or whoever he was, nodded them through. Her father stood up, visibly moved at the sight of Sam. He limped forward. Limping? What had happened to him?

He opened his arms. 'My little girl. I thought I'd lost you.'

Sam hesitated only for a moment before responding. Jess breathed a relieved sigh, realising that she had been holding her breath. It was going to be all right. Sam was going to accept him — and forgive.

Sam drew back first. Her voice was quavering a little. 'Jess said you needed to see us all together.'

'Yes, of course. Sorry to get emotional. I've hoped for this, so much. So many years wasted.' The other three said nothing. 'Well, sit down. They've found some chairs.'

In spite of all her resolve, Jess could hold back no longer. 'Who? Who are these people?'

'Yes, I know. I'll begin at the beginning.' He closed his eyes, brushed a hand across his forehead. 'Your mother and I had three children, the three of you, in quick succession. I had severe money problems at the time; I'd made some ill-advised investments. I only wanted to provide for you all. When — let's say, a friend — suggested another way of acquiring money, it seemed the obvious solution. Done very cleverly so it wouldn't be missed. Amazing how figures can be adjusted without anyone noticing.'

'So it worked?' Jess said, keeping her voice neutral. She was aware that Sam had gasped.

'Of course.'

Jess said, 'Whose money is it?'

Her father shrugged impatiently. 'It doesn't matter now. It was a long time ago. So long ago that now I can retrieve it, also without anyone noticing. It's good news. We're made. Secure for life. You three as well, naturally. We just have to reclaim it.'

Jess said slowly, 'Right. Where from?' She knew her father too well. Any sign of disapproval, and he would clam up and they would learn nothing. 'And I don't quite get what you mean.' He was making it all sound far too simple. She wasn't convinced.

'That's where you come in. We all knew, my friends and I, that we would have to wait for some time before it was safe to reclaim all of it. We just took the minimum needed to restore our situations. But it became obvious that I couldn't trust the others. And they seemed to think the same, so we came to our solution: no one person would know where the money was.'

Sam said, 'I don't understand.'

'I expect the information was split,' Jess said. 'You all knew *something*, but not all of it.'

Her father smiled. 'I knew you would follow me.'

'And you want us to chase after these pieces of info and find it for you?'

Oliver said suddenly, 'You're still dancing around it, aren't you? You just can't bring yourself to tell the girls the truth. Even though you have every intention of using the three of us again — because let's face it, you have from the start.' He took a step forward. 'We have the information. It was stored on three microchips, like vets use for dogs and cats. And they were injected into the three of us. Into our hands. Into the fleshy part between the thumb and index finger.'

Sam's face was horrified. 'No! We must have been babies. Or very small.'

Jess said, 'What? That can't be right. I would have known. Wouldn't I?' She spread her palms, staring at them.

Oliver said, 'Oh, that's where it went slightly askew. When I broke my thumb last year and needed an X-ray, I was told about a foreign body that had been detected. And I started putting things together. Being older than you two, I could remember bits of what had happened at the time, when our father made the decision to use us. To him, we were no more than domestic pets.'

Their father said mildly, 'That isn't quite fair. But Oliver sought me out. And, of course, for all his seeming objections, is on board.'

Jess raised her eyebrows. But why was she surprised? She'd always thought her brother knew more than he was telling her.

Sam said quietly, 'Animals are very important to a lot of people. Part of the family, as much as humans are.'

Their father gave her an approving nod. 'Of course. And it was a dangerous situation. There were disagreements, threats of violence. And when my wife — '

Oliver interrupted: ' — decided she'd had enough of it and tried to escape with the three of us, things came to a head.'

Leo Dryden shook his head. 'You're right. The worst thing she could have done. But the others saw what she was doing. She sped off with you, Sam, and I haven't seen you since. A great sorrow to me.'

Jess said, 'Leaving me and Oliver behind.'

He sighed. 'I had no idea she was going to do that. It was the *other* group members who saw you as commodities, able to carry the chips, rather than human beings. Not me.'

Jess sighed. 'And whose fault was that? We were *your* children. It *was* up to you.'

'It was a very dangerous situation. This was the only way I could placate them. I had to get them to calm down, take back the violent threats, and put their guns away. I had to assure them I would find Sam, and I had to give Oliver to — '

Oliver's face was dark. 'Franklin. The man who adopted me — and with your encouragement. Thanks. Not a good choice.'

'I know. You can't believe how sorry I am. But I counted myself fortunate that I'd been able to keep Jess.'

Jess stared at him. Some of this was true, certainly. But she doubted whether all of it could be. She had discovered in the last week how easily her father could twist things when it suited him. Would there even be any point in asking how the plan had been supposed to pan out at the time? In her experience, he would

162

have a convoluted explanation for every query.

What mattered was what was going to happen now. How were they to get out of all of this?

She said, 'So, as I see it, you need the information from our three chips to satisfy these mysterious people who are keeping you here — and that will be it. All sorted.'

'Exactly. Thanks, Jess. I knew you'd understand.' He smiled round at all of them.

Sam said, 'Just a minute. Whose money is it? Was it?'

Their father said quickly, 'That doesn't matter now. As I said, it was a long time ago.'

'It isn't yours, though, is it?'

There was a silence before he said, 'Maybe it belonged to a great many people, in comparatively small amounts, who haven't missed it. But, hands on the table, you're right. It isn't a black and white situation. Some of the people we removed it from were hardly angels.

And, of course, that's why many of them never complained.' He nodded at Sam. 'But I can see you're not happy about it, just like your mother couldn't see things sensibly at the time.' He sat back. 'So, I'll tell you what. When we have retrieved it, we can see about giving it back. We can discuss it, all together. We won't do anything you're not happy with.'

*But if he's being coerced*, Jess thought, *how can he promise that?*

Sam's voice was normally soft, but now, suddenly, she was loud and defiant. 'No. I don't believe you. If you've done what you said — if you could think it was okay to insert a chip into me when we were so small, which led to us being split up — how can I accept anything you say? No. I'm not agreeing. You can't have the information from my chip. The whole thing is wicked. And I don't much care what happens to you, if that part's true. It's your own fault and you must take the consequences.'

Oliver and Jess were both staring at

her, Oliver half-smiling. Jess thought, *Wow!* Half-admiring, but half in annoyance. It would have been so easy to go along with it and have done, but Sam was right. Jess had underestimated her. She had seemed so soft and gentle and unassuming, but she had inherited her share of the family fire and determination.

Their father said, 'It seems I've been taking too much for granted. I thought you would be sensible — like the other two. But then, you've had unfortunate influences.'

Jess was now thinking, *Hang on*. 'No. I can't go along with this either.'

Their father's voice was low and angry. 'Even though I've told you what will happen to me if you don't co-operate?'

Jess said, 'That's just it, Dad. You haven't told us. Just hinted. Who are these people?'

He sat back. 'Far better if you didn't know — but okay, I'll spell it out for you. There were four of us in the original group. We all agreed to let the trail go cold before accessing the money, which took longer than some of us expected. We couldn't agree on the exact timings. These were ruthless men.' He shrugged sadly. 'Maybe I was wrong to enter in with them.'

'Why is now the right time?'

'Ah, things have changed. The others have all died — one quite recently — so there's no need to worry about them. And Oliver brought me the sad news of Franklin's death. That's right, isn't it, Oliver?'

Oliver said nothing.

Jess raised her eyebrows. Oliver hadn't even mentioned that.

Leo Dryden was nodding. 'One was a vet. He thought of the chipping idea, and had the equipment. One was an expert with figures and finance. He came up with our original . . . venture . . . in the first place. Very clever. He discovered a dubious scheme set up by someone else, and worked out a way to siphon the ill-gotten gains off to an account in our names.'

Sam said, 'Why didn't you just report this other person to the police?'

'We were in crisis. I thought I'd explained that. We'd invested heavily in a business plan that seemed foolproof. But it failed, and left us all desperate to recoup our losses. We just wanted enough to get back on track. And we ended up with more than we needed.'

'And what did you do with the extra?' Jess asked quietly.

Dryden paused. 'In a foreign account. Your chips contain the account details.'

'You could still give it back, surely?'

'What, after all this time? Impossible to trace the original owners, the ones who acquired it dishonestly.'

'You could give it to charity,' Sam said.

It was as if something snapped. The affable manner disappeared. 'I told you we could discuss that later. We're wasting time.'

Sam said, 'No. I want to know what's going to happen before we do anything else.'

There was fury in Leo Dryden's face. 'I can't let you leave until I have it.' He stood up, clicking his fingers to the man at the door. 'You'll have to stay here, Sam, until you change your mind. You won't be too uncomfortable.'

Sam said, 'But I won't change it.'

He ignored her. 'You can stay with her, Jess. I'm sure you can persuade her. But don't be too long. Things could start getting unpleasant.'

# 13

The room emptied. The two women heard the door shut behind them, and a key turn in the lock. They stared at each other.

Jess said, 'I can't believe what just happened. How could he do that? Sam, he isn't like that.' She knew she was trying to convince herself. She was no longer sure what her father was like. Or what he was capable of.

'Where's Oliver? Why has *he* left the room with the others?'

'I don't know.' Jess was reaching for her phone. 'No reception.' But who would she have rung? 'He's been helpful to me today but I've only just met him. He's an unknown quantity.'

'Like our father is to me,' Sam said quietly, 'I'm afraid you won't change my mind, Jess. This is wrong.'

'Of course. I'm not even going to try.'

'Just as my mother always said. Our father can't be trusted.'

'I suppose he was left in a difficult position.'

'He could at least have told you the truth. How could he have ever told you our mother was dead? That's wicked.'

Jess put her hands to her face, resting her elbows on her knees. 'I was already doubting him.' She thought grimly, *Ever since he led me to someone else's gravestone and faked a heart attack. Even before that, maybe.*

Sam said, 'I don't think he's a very nice person.'

'Maybe not. But he's our father all the same.'

'It's his own fault if I can't feel any loyalty to him. And *love*, that's too much to ask. Mum didn't do anything like that. I knew *he* was still alive.'

Jess said slowly, 'If she'd ever tried to find me, his claim would have been shown to be a lie, wouldn't it? But she can't have done.'

Sam sighed. 'I suppose so. But I think

she was afraid of him. I don't know what she thought about you or Oliver. Like I said, she never even mentioned you. Too painful, I expect.'

'Mm. Looks like there's been wrong done on both sides, to me.'

'When I see her again, I'll ask her about it.' Sam bit her lip.

'And that's the thing, isn't it? Neither of us is going anywhere. We're stuck here. We have to escape.'

Sam smiled. 'Oh, good. Because I won't back down.'

'I know. I won't either. And you're right, the whole thing stinks. Assuming we can believe even half of what he's telling us.'

'So we have to get out of here.' Sam looked round. 'It's very secure.'

'Yes.' Jess climbed up onto the bed and shook at the barred half-window by the ceiling. 'No, they're not even rusted. Totally firm.'

'I don't think we could get through even if they were loose.'

'I know. I was thinking that if we

were looking out onto the street, we could try and attract someone's attention. But we're onto the yard at the back.'

'We'll have to think of something else. What about the door?' Sam stepped towards it.

'No,' Jess said quickly. 'Don't shake it. We heard them lock it. Don't let them think we're trying it.'

'Why not?'

'Better if they think we're sitting here quietly with me trying to persuade you.'

Sam sat down. 'We shouldn't have tried the window then. Perhaps they can see us. There may be a camera.' She looked round, lowering her voice. 'Seems odd to me, this. We're as good as imprisoned, so why is he seeking our agreement? We couldn't agree to the chips being inserted, could we? He only needs to wait until we're asleep, slip us a sleeping tablet even, and he can get the chip scanned whenever he likes.' She paused. 'Unless, yes, Mum was right. He's always been a control freak.

No achievement in just taking the information. I have to be moulded to his will and give it to him voluntarily.' She shivered.

'Probably. I think we have to accept it's unlikely we can get out of here on our own. And work on from there.'

Sam said bitterly, 'He's too organised. He has far too many underlings around.'

Jess nodded, sitting beside her. 'Including Oliver.' Who had obviously betrayed them. And why shouldn't he? Yes, he was their brother; there were enough small family resemblances to leave her in no doubt of it. But he didn't know them, had been discarded by both parents as if he didn't matter. Why should any of his real family matter to *him*? She said, 'Did you know we had a brother, Sam?'

'Mum said something once or twice that made me think there might be. But when I asked her, she wouldn't say.'

'When I first met him, I was wary of him, but I was beginning to trust him.'

Perhaps that had been the idea.

'He seems to be firmly on our father's side now.'

'Doesn't he just? That's what makes me think it's all been part of a plan.'

'To gain your trust,' Sam said.

'Something like that.' Jess lowered her voice still further. 'Listen, I think we should pretend to be going along with it. There may be a better chance to escape later.'

'But if we do that, our father will have the bank details and go straight for the stolen money. How will we have any control over what he does next? We want to return it, don't we? And if there are so many people involved, far better to hand it over to the police. Let them sort it out.'

Jess took a deep breath. 'I'm sorry, Sam, but that means handing him over too. I'm not certain I'm ready to do that. And I can't see that the police will ever trace where it's from either. Donating it to charity seems the best option.'

Sam paused. 'Maybe,' she said doubtfully. 'I just don't want to give up on the idea of returning it if there's any chance at all.'

'Anyway, we're not making sense. We need to know where it is and how much there is. How about if we allow him to read our chips? And then get them read ourselves as soon as we can. Then we can decide what to do next. Perhaps even get to the account first somehow.'

Sam paused, thinking. 'You're making it sound so easy. But okay, I can see that's probably the best plan. All we've got. There's no point in my having high principles if I'm stuck here forever.'

'It wouldn't be forever,' Jess said quickly.

'Really? Well, you know him better than I do. But trusting a man who could involve his infant children in this scheme in the first place? Who knows what he might do?'

Jess wanted to leap to his defence. Normally, she would have done. Fiery, feisty Jess would have done just that.

But if Sam could be sensible, so could she. They needed to get out of here. She sighed. 'Perhaps.'

'So how are *we* going to get these chips read anyway? For when we *are* out of here?'

Jess said, trying to be brisk, 'I expect we need a vet. We could find one on the internet.'

Sam said, 'Nat's father was a vet, I think. I'm sure he's mentioned that.'

'Nat?'

'You met him. At the café in Roundhay Park.' She was half-smiling.

Jess looked at her. 'I remember. And he's important to you, isn't he?'

'Yes, you're right. But I'm not sure — well, never mind. The point is, he may be able to help us.'

'You're right. That could be useful.' Jess hoped she sounded positive; was this too convenient? She had a niggling sense of unease. Hadn't her father just told them that one of the gang members had been a vet? 'Where is he now?'

'He said he would follow on when we left with Oliver.' Sam brightened. 'So as soon as we have phone reception again, he'll come and help us.'

'As soon as we get out of here. Okay, then. So you're with me on this? We'll go along with it?' She spoke more loudly, in case anyone was listening.

'As long as we can go to the bank or wherever it is, along with your father. It's no good if we just let him read the chips and then leave us here,' Sam said quickly.

Jess nodded. Worth a try. 'You're right. Okay.' She swivelled her eyes toward the door and Sam nodded back. Jess walked over and knocked loudly. 'Hey! Hello? We're ready to talk to someone now.'

A pause, and then a deep laugh. 'Mr Dryden doesn't think you've been there long enough.'

'Well, we have. Would you tell him, please?'

'He's not available right now.'

Jess laughed. 'No, he wouldn't be.

Why am I not surprised?'

'He's playing with us,' Sam said.

'Of course he is. But I think he *is* available and will get the message. No way he wouldn't get it. Dad likes to know what's going on.'

'So we wait.'

'Yes.'

They were silent for a few minutes. Sam whispered, 'Will he believe us?'

'I've always wanted to know about our mother. And now I do know, he won't feel certain of how I might react to any of this.'

'I suppose creating uncertainty in your enemy is better than nothing.'

Jess winced. In spite of everything, she could never think of her father as an enemy. If she were ever to bring her father and sister together with some kind of amity, she had a great deal of work to do. 'Let's just get out of this room and start talking to him and see what happens. Play things by ear. But Sam, if I get a sudden idea and seem to be going off at a tangent, try and play along with me.' She added, 'And I'll do the same for you.'

'I don't think that's too likely. And what time is it? He may intend on leaving us here all night — until we think he's forgotten about us.' Sam paused. 'Perhaps we should take turns at trying to sleep. You can have the bed first.'

Jess hardly thought sleep would be possible, but she was wearier than she realised from her ordeal of the previous night. She must have drifted off almost at once before suddenly she was waking abruptly, limbs cold and stiff as she heard a key turning in the lock. Sam gave a suppressed squeak.

Jess said, trying to sound reassuring, 'And about time. We could do with something to eat, too.'

The door opened.

# 14

Jess gasped. They were looking at Oliver. He said quietly, 'Come on. There's nobody about now. It's safe.'

'Safe?' Jess hissed. 'How can it be? You betrayed us.'

'No, I didn't — but there's no time for that now. Do you want to get out of here or not?'

'Yes, we do,' Sam said firmly. She was already past Jess and joining Oliver in the doorway.

'We don't know whether we can trust him,' Jess muttered. But Sam was right. No point in staying here.

The corridor outside was dark and quiet. Too quiet and too easy. Wasn't it? Jess followed Oliver, with Sam now close behind her. She could hear Sam's breathing clearly, too loud and too fast. Perhaps hers sounded just as bad.

They were taking a different route to

the way they had come in. Was that a good thing or not? They came to another set of badly-lit and cold stairs. Before she had expected it, there was frosty air on their faces.

'This way,' Oliver said.

'Where's your car?'

'We don't need it.' They were out on the street. Further down another car was moving towards them, coming to a halt on the double yellow lines. As if this whole move had been planned. What plan? Whose? Had they exchanged one danger for another?

Oliver seized one of the door handles. 'Come on, quickly.'

'Hang on a minute.'

But Jess's objection was swamped by Sam's gleeful, 'Oh, Nat! You found us.'

The driver was grinning at her. 'I never lost you.'

The girls tumbled onto the rear seat with Oliver in the front. Why was he coming too, and where were they going? Sam obviously didn't care.

But someone had to. 'I knew it,' Jess

snapped. 'You're involved too. What's going on?'

'Let's just get out of here — and then we'll tell you,' Nat said.

Oliver said, 'When we're at a safe distance.'

But safe for who? Next to Jess, Sam whispered, 'It's okay now. You'll see.'

Jess muttered, 'I wish I could think so.' But there was no point in making any further objections. Oliver and this Nat held all the cards just now. Oliver who she doubted could be trusted; and Nat, whose father must have been a part of it from the beginning. Allowing Sam to vouch for him was hardly a sound idea; Sam was obviously blinded by her emotions.

Jess sighed. She should follow her own advice, but there was just too much playing things by ear and adjusting to the moment for her liking.

Pay attention. She should be taking notice of their direction now. They were moving out of the city centre, but she hadn't been watching the route and didn't recognise the rows of semi-detached houses. Nat pulled in to park by some playing fields.

'Where are we?' Jess demanded.

'Haven't a clue, but there's nobody else around. And we need to read the chips, don't we?' Nat said.

'Only with your full agreement and co-operation of course,' Oliver added. Was he being sincere?

Sam was looking round too. 'I don't know. There are a couple of dog walkers in the distance and a jogger over there. Somebody might wonder what we're doing, parked here at this time in the morning. A bit soon to be getting the beers out, and we haven't a dog.'

'People mind their own business,' Oliver said.

Nat said cheerfully, 'They'll probably think we're drug dealers and give us a wide berth.'

'Really?'

Nat leaned back and patted Sam's hand. 'I wasn't being serious but it's quite likely. Lucky for us.'

Oliver was turning round too. 'Let's just get on with it, shall we? Franklin had mine removed when the medics found it. I have it now.'

Sam said, 'He just gave it to you?'

'He died.'

'Oh, yes. I remember now. I'm sorry.'

Jess frowned. There was something about the way he'd said it; a chill of unease had trickled across her neck. 'Was his death sudden?'

'Makes no difference. Scanner, Nat?'

'I suppose not,' Jess muttered. Neither of the others seemed to have noticed anything.

'Yep. Here it is. And here's a notepad for you two; write the numbers down when I read them out.'

'Got that.' Jess said. 'So, what do we have to do now?'

Oliver opened his palm, revealing a piece of card. 'Start with this one, Nat.'

The girls both leaned forward. Sam said, 'That's amazing. You can hardly see it. If you didn't have it taped to that cardboard, you might have lost it.'

Oliver laughed. 'No chance.'

Jess wrote his numbers down. Did this mean they could trust him? She'd wondered whether he would hang back until theirs had been read, then do a runner without sharing his. She said, 'If they're injected in the first place, they would have to be small.'

'Sorry, yes. I wasn't thinking.'

Nat said, 'Just pass your left hand over here, between the seats. We'll try that one first.'

Sam obeyed. 'All the same, I can hardly believe I never knew it was there.'

'You'd be surprised how many people have chips in their hands, purposely. There's an idea on the go that if they could somehow have one injected with their travel card info on it, they could just waft their hand when catching the tube instead of inserting the card. But I don't think anyone has been successful yet. Okay, here we go. Did you get that, Jess?'

'Yes.' She passed the notepad to Sam,

and they exchanged hands.

Oliver was drumming his fingers on the sill. 'Get on with it. Is it there or not?'

'Could have moved, you know,' Nat said mildly. 'But it's here.'

Jess was quietly copying both sets of numbers to another page, and gently tearing it out. Best to leave nothing to chance. She said, 'I was expecting a longer sequence of numbers.'

Oliver said, 'So was I.'

Jess read them again. 'And I thought that Sam's might have some extra significance, since my father made so much effort to get hold of her. But it doesn't seem any different. Look, Sam. This is why everyone's been chasing you.'

To her surprise, Sam was staring at the page with a horrified expression, her eyes filling with tears. She said, 'That's it, isn't it, Nat? That's why you came into my life so suddenly? You lied to me.'

Jess gripped her arm. Where on earth

was all this coming from? And from Sam, who always seemed to see the sunny side and the best in everyone. She said, 'That can't be right. Don't get upset.'

Sam said, 'I always knew I'd been so very lucky to meet you. Almost too lucky. I couldn't believe it. Or why you should be interested in me. And now I know — my instincts were right all along.'

Nat made no attempt to deny it. 'I'm sorry. In the first place, yes. Leo Dryden employed me to find you and watch out for you. But as soon as I'd met you, I began to care for you for yourself. I watched out for you as instructed, but I didn't pass on the information. Or take the payments. Please believe me, Sam.'

'But why did you leave me so suddenly, without explaining? Why did you come up here?'

'Because I cared too much about you. Because I didn't want you to have anything to do with all this. It was becoming too dangerous. I wanted you right out of it.'

Jess glared at him. Did that make sense? She supposed so, reluctantly.

Sam, it seemed, was accepting his belated explanation more readily. 'I think I can understand that. If you cared for me.' She smiled, tearfully. 'But I came blundering in anyway. I expect I've spoiled everything.'

Nat grinned. 'No. That's my girl. I should have realised you would.'

Sam said, 'All the same — '

Oliver said briskly, 'You can sort your romantic life out later at your leisure. Let's see these numbers.' His voice was rising.

'Okay, okay,' Nat said easily. 'After all this time, a few more minutes won't make any difference. What have we got, Jess?'

She passed the notepad through to the front seats. 'I've taken a copy for myself.' How would Oliver react to that?

He just said, 'Good. So did I.'

*So far, so good*, Jess thought. 'That

doesn't look like a bank code to me. It's too short.'

Sam said, 'Wouldn't bank codes have been shorter back then, maybe? Everything was less complicated, wasn't it?'

'I don't think so. And the first part should be a sort code, followed by an account number, but it doesn't look right.' Jess frowned. 'We need a sort code to know what bank we're talking about. Otherwise where do we start? Or maybe some other person has that?'

'No way. There are only the three of us. This stinks,' Oliver said forcefully. 'None of it makes sense.'

'You're right,' Jess agreed. 'Anyway, we would need a password to access it, wouldn't we?'

'Not at a branch. And especially not back then. But the account will be dormant anyway if no one has used it for years. The bank, whichever it is, should have written to the account holders and said so.'

Jess said, 'I don't think they always do that.'

'This is nothing to do with any bank,' Oliver said, his voice still hard. 'It's something entirely different. He's lied to us. Again.'

'Come on,' Nat said equably. 'You can't be that surprised.'

'No,' Jess agreed, swallowing hard. No point in sticking up for him, although she felt as if she'd been punched in the heart. 'We just need to work out what else it might be.' She stared at the sequence of numbers.

'They're a bit like the numbers for our burglar alarm,' Sam proffered.

Jess said, 'Yes, something shorter. Or a safe combination.'

'Yes!' Oliver said. 'I'll bet it is. Well done.'

Jess was looking at him through narrowed eyes, not sure that she believed in his reaction. 'But that doesn't get us any nearer, does it? What safe? Where is it?'

Oliver said nothing, but his fingers were drumming again, this time on his knee. As if he'd come up with something and didn't intend to share it.

Sam said, 'We have to think back to when this all first happened.'

Nat laughed suddenly. 'Of course we do. So let's go.'

# 15

Jess said again, 'Where are we going?'

She wasn't expecting a reply. Oliver and Nat glanced at each other. Oliver nodded, almost imperceptibly.

'Will you stop this?' Jess demanded. 'Tell us.'

Nat grinned. 'I know. Sorry. We're going to Quarry House.' He paused, as if waiting for one of the sisters to respond to that.

Jess frowned. Yes. Something in her memory was pinging. That was a name she had heard before. She said, 'Is that your house?'

Almost simultaneously, Sam was saying, 'Is that where you live?'

'Yes to your question, Jess. No to yours, Sam. It's not fit for habitation at present.'

Pictures were seeping into her mind. Jess said slowly, 'Did we live there too?

Or maybe we didn't actually live there. Were we on holiday? Is it out in the country somewhere?'

Nat laughed, and yet there was bitterness in his voice. 'Not exactly the countryside, even then. But it must have seemed like it to you. Has a big garden, and not far from the park.'

'We must be nearly there.'

Sam said, 'So I already knew you, years ago. But why were we living with you?'

'Our fathers knew each other.'

'Were they friends?' Sam asked.

'Not exactly. Business colleagues, you might say. And you were staying with us temporarily. Because we had plenty of room, my dad said. That's how he was. A good man. Generous to his friends — and had too many of them. Hopeless with money.'

'Was?' Jess said cautiously. Nat's voice seemed calm, but that bitterness was still there.

'Yes, my parents died last year. You might call it an accident.'

'Oh,' Jess said. 'I'm sorry.' Sam was leaning forward, her face hidden by her hair. She would know this already, Jess thought. Another chill crossed her neck. Why had so many of her father's old friends and business associates met with accidents?

Her throat felt tight. No. Surely not. No, no, no. It couldn't possibly be anything to do with him. He wouldn't. How could she even be thinking that? She was seeing criminal acts where none existed. Her father might be devious and control-seeking, but that was all. Wasn't it?

They were driving along a residential tree-lined street, turning off down a long drive backed with overgrown rhododendrons. Pulling up in a large circular space where weeds grew through the gravel, in front of a large detached house.

Jess gasped. She knew it. She remembered. Those dark shrubs and a car parked almost where they were now. Waiting in the open doorway of the house with Oliver holding her hand, watching as their mother strapped Sam into the back of the car. They had to be quiet. Oliver was pulling at her hand and saying, 'Ssh. Ssh.' Fiercely. Jess knew she had to be quiet, but she couldn't help it. She started to cry.

And suddenly they were surrounded by dark, tall figures. There was noise and angry shouting. Her mother's white face as she turned in panic, slammed shut the car door, leapt into the front seat and drove off. With Sam. The last time Jess had seen either of them, until now.

She swallowed. 'It was here.'

For the first time, she looked up at the house. Or, what had once been a spacious and elegant building. Now it was half-ruined. To the left of the front door, the stone frontage seemed almost intact; the rest was a blackened shell.

She felt dazed. She realised that she was gripping Sam's hand, too tightly. She muttered 'Sorry' as she let go.

Sam said nothing. She seemed

shocked too, although surely she would have been too young to remember.

Nat said, 'A gas explosion, apparently. I can rebuild, or demolish and start again. When the insurance is sorted out. That's proving a problem, as you might expect.'

No one else spoke. Jess had to ask. 'Why? You don't mean — you don't think — It *was* a gas explosion, wasn't it?'

'Oh, yes. Even the experts seem to think so. But it did cross my mind that it could have been convenient for somebody.'

'You mean, my father,' Jess said, knowing that her voice was bitter now. But not knowing whether her anger was directed at Nat or her father.

'Sorry, Jess. Yes. Although I could be wrong. Because the outcome hasn't actually turned out to be that convenient, has it?' He shook his head. 'Unless someone was thinking my dad would be out of the running for collecting his share. The group didn't need his specialist knowledge any more. I have his scanner, but they'll be available on the internet now. All the same, easier to give him his share and be done with it; rather than go through all this hassle and still get nowhere.'

'So, okay. Let's say there was no advantage in the death of your parents.' Jess almost spat the words at him. 'So why say it? Why even think it? You're not being fair.' She glared at him in the driving mirror. She could see his eyes.

Nat shrugged. 'It's not that simple, even so. There are one or two things my father said, not long before he died. Things he started to tell me — and then seemed to change his mind, not having said quite enough, but giving me the idea that something was wrong. Unfortunately, I didn't take enough notice at the time. I should have pressed him. Dad did tend to worry about stuff for no reason. I just thought this was more of the same. More fool me.'

Sam said suddenly, 'But what if the

explosion wasn't intended to hurt anyone? Perhaps that number did belong to a safe, and someone wanted to search for it — or *had* found it and needed to blow it open?'

Nat said quietly, 'The effect was the same. They're still dead. But I see what you mean, Sam. It's easier to live with an accident than deliberate murder.'

Jess said, 'If the explosion uncovered the safe, then whoever caused the explosion will have taken it, surely? And that's not my father, because obviously he's still looking for it.' She knew she sounded triumphant, and that it was hardly appropriate considering what had happened to Nat's parents, but she couldn't help it. Her relief was over-whelming.

'Oh, I agree,' Nat said. 'Anyone could have taken it. There were boundless opportunities. As you can see, the wreckage of the house is hardly blocked off securely. No problem at all getting through those rickety steel fences. I can get in any time I want. And straight afterwards, there were experts swarming all over it. There could have been any number of extra unauthorised visits, and I wouldn't have known.' His voice dropped a little. 'Or cared, at the time.'

'But, like I said, not my dad.'

'No. Though I'm sure he came up and had a good look. Even now it's all quietened down, I don't know who comes and goes. I live in a flat over the garage, round the other side. And I agree, your father is still looking. In fact, I know he is.'

Simultaneously, Jess said, 'You see!' and Sam said quietly, 'How?'

Oliver said nothing, although Nat had turned to look at him directly.

Nat said, 'Because the safe is still here.'

# 16

Jess tried to process Nat's surprising statement. She found herself staring at the back of Oliver's neck, aware of how the muscles beneath his hairline had tightened. She was certain that he was controlling his responses with a supreme effort of will.

Was that why Nat had chosen this dramatic way of relaying the information? To see how they would react — and Oliver in particular? Did this mean Nat also didn't trust Oliver?

Sam said, 'And you know where it is?'

'I do. Shall we go and have a look?'

None of them moved. Jess said, 'Is it dangerous?' She wasn't sure what kind of danger she was expecting. The building collapsing? Yet another betrayal? Considering both Nat and Oliver, she would trust Oliver the most; but all the same — She only had Sam's perception to go on that Nat could be trusted, and by now Sam might have changed her mind. Though his explanations and regret concerning how they'd met had seemed convincing.

Jess glanced sideways at Sam. Had she been quieter than usual since Nat's unwelcome revelations? Hard to say whether her feelings for him had altered. Love could make people do strange things.

Nat said, 'Don't be too worried by the barriers. This side of the house is okay. I can go in and out whenever I like without anything falling on me or going through the floorboards. No problem at all. But, as I said, I can't rebuild until I have the verdict for the insurance.'

There was no way of disproving that. Jess said, 'It's taking a long time, isn't it? Surely the experts can be very accurate these days?' She wanted to gauge his reaction to her doubts.

'Oh, I'm sure they do know by now.

Or have a very good idea. But they're not keen to part with the money too quickly, so they're in no hurry to say.'

Jess nodded. They got out of the car.

Nat seemed to be the only one willing to say anything. 'Do you three remember that night? I don't of course. I was tucked up safely in bed, and didn't hear a thing. But your mum told me about it, Sam.'

If he had wanted to get a reaction from Sam, he had been successful. Her voice was shocked. 'My mum? I didn't know you'd met her.'

'Yes.' Nat stopped.

Jess narrowed her eyes as she watched him, every sense newly alert. Already he was regretting saying that, she was certain of it. Sam was tense. She must have picked up on that too.

Sam said, 'I see it now. It was all because of Mum, wasn't it? And what she told you? That's why you left so suddenly.'

'Sam, I had to, when she told me the whole truth about what had happened and I realised how dangerous this could be. I'd already decided that allowing myself to be recruited by Leo Dryden wasn't right; I was considering giving him notice. But now I knew I'd badly misjudged the situation. I had to go, and fast — and in such a way that he wouldn't know where you were.'

Jess knew that Sam would erupt at any moment, in anger or tears or both. She could hardly blame her, but there wasn't time for all that. She put a hand on Sam's wrist — to calm her, she hoped. 'So did she tell you, Nat? What really happened that night? When we were small. What was her viewpoint on it?'

Nat took a long slow breath. 'That's right. She did tell me. This is where her car was parked, on the drive at the front of the house, ready to go. And she had the three of you all dressed and ready in the hall. I suppose, with Sam being the smallest, she loaded her first; strapping her into the front seat would take a few minutes. It was raining, she said.

Otherwise she would have let you wait outside. One small decision, and one she's regretted for the rest of her life.'

Oliver spoke suddenly, in that expressionless voice, as if reading aloud. 'She told me to be very quiet and look after Jess. I could hear the men talking in the sitting room. I wanted to follow, whatever our mother had said, and even though it was raining so hard.'

'Yes,' Jess breathed, staring at the house. 'I remember too. You were pulling at my hand, Oliver, but Mum had said to keep still so I was cross with you and wouldn't go. And then an argument started in the sitting room.'

Oliver turned and looked straight at Jess with accusation in his cold eyes. 'They were shouting.'

'Yes. I was frightened. Terrified.'

'And you let out a wail. Louder than any noise they were making. They stopped. There was one long moment of silence, and then they all came running out. And our mother left us. She was still out by the car, and she piled into the driver's seat and drove off.'

Sam said softly, 'I suppose she panicked.'

Oliver made a contemptuous sound. 'An unfortunate reaction. Not too bad for Jess, as it turned out, but very unfortunate for me.'

'But you have forgiven Mum, haven't you?' Sam pleaded. 'She must have regretted it so much. She never told me about any of this, but I know she was very unhappy.'

'She didn't try to get us back though, did she?'

Jess said, 'We don't know. Maybe she did.' Poor woman, driven by fear and loss. She was wondering, however, just how hard their mother had tried. Because much as Jess loved her father, she knew how terrifying he could be when crossed. The force of that anger had never fully been directed at her; she had been fortunate enough to be loved and idolised by him, but she had seen enough of his fury to recognise that it was to be avoided.

There was an awkward pause. Sam said, 'Oliver?'

'Yeah. Of course I've forgiven her. What else? Why hang around? They were dangerous men. She wasn't to know that I would be handed over to one of the worst of them. And no doubt, at the time, she told herself she would come back for us. But I didn't see any signs of it.'

'Didn't you move around a lot?' Sam said eagerly. 'As if you were trying to avoid someone? We did.'

'Only when it was needful for that man's job.'

'But surely — ' Sam was beginning.

'Okay,' Nat said. 'Let's deal with now and what we've come for. This used to be the front door, but as you can see, it's out of action. I've had to board it up. We can get in round the back.'

Jess and Sam were opening their car doors, but Oliver didn't move. He said abruptly, 'What's the point? There's nothing left of the room where they were all arguing that night, the room containing the safe.'

Jess frowned. How did he know all this? How could Oliver know where the safe was? Unless Franklin had told him. But why would he volunteer that information? He would want to benefit from that knowledge himself. She shivered. Maybe the man had been made to tell Oliver. One way or another.

Nat was saying, 'If the safe had still been there, the supposed gas explosion would have blown it open. Exposed it, at least. My parents were sleeping in the room directly above, and that's when they were killed.'

Sam and Jess both murmured something. Nat continued as if he hadn't noticed. 'But it wasn't there. My dad had decided to move it. He thought it would be more secure that way. Somehow, he just didn't trust the others. A few years ago, my parents had some extensive alterations done here: a two-storey extension, a couple of en suites in the main house. One weekend when the builders weren't here, my dad took the opportunity to move the safe. It wasn't difficult for him; he was pretty good at DIY anyway.'

They followed Nat round past the leaning metal barriers; which as Nat had said, were only at the front of the building.

Once, Jess thought, it must have been a beautiful house. Looking out onto an extensive lawn surrounded by shrubs and flower borders. Winding paths and overgrown hedges and rockeries. Someone, presumably Nat, had kept up with the lawn, but the rest was beginning to show a wild neglect. A wonderful place to be a child, and no doubt Nat and his parents had been happy here. Before his father had become entangled with Leo Dryden.

She sighed. How could you be so close to someone through all the years of growing up, and yet have no idea of who he really was? Perhaps, deep inside, she had always known and closed her eyes to it. He was her dad and she loved him; what else could she do?

*Snap out of that*, she told herself. She shook her head in annoyance. Concentrate on what had to be done now. Nat was right.

They were making their way through the undamaged part at the rear of the house where there was a vast, empty kitchen diner. 'We're using the back stairs,' Nat said, 'originally intended for the servants, fortunately for us. The main stairs aren't too safe anymore. I've used them occasionally but there are too many of us to risk it.'

'You can't tell there's even been an explosion here,' Sam said. They were standing on an inner landing, faced with several closed doors.

'It does look okay. But even here, the doors don't open too well. Everything's out of kilter.' Nat chose the nearest door and pulled the handle towards himself and upwards, giving a heave with his shoulder at the same time.

Jess said, 'Wouldn't it be easier to

leave them open?'

'I suspect they're supporting whatever's above them. It could make things worse. It's easy enough when you have the knack.'

The room was still furnished as a bedroom, but sparsely. It had a neglected, unlived-in feel. Worse, Jess thought, than the rooms that were empty.

Nat said, 'This is the room I had when I lived here, and when I came back to stay with them. I've moved everything of mine out now, obviously.'

'It's still panelled,' Oliver said. 'But it was never this light.'

'Yes. Too dark then, my mum always said. She loved it when we had it painted.' He smiled. 'My dad said the pale green would make the house look like an upmarket pub, but she got her way in the end.'

Sam sighed. 'Oh, Nat, your dad sounds lovely.'

Oliver said, 'The panelling would be good for concealing a safe.'

'That's right.'

'Do we have to start tapping around the whole room looking for secret panels?' As he spoke, Oliver was already examining the panelling, opening and closing cupboard doors that, from where Jess was standing, were almost invisible. Wherever it was, it had been very cleverly done.

Nat said, 'Be my guest.' He was grinning. 'I doubt if you'll find it.'

Oliver flashed him a look of brief antagonism before returning to his customary calm expression. 'And you know where it is?'

'Of course.'

'I'm sure this is all very entertaining for you. Enjoying your moment of triumph and power — but could we get on with it?'

Jess looked at him, but he was keeping his emotions in check now. 'There's no hurry,' she said quietly. Or was there? Oliver had been edgy all along. More than seemed necessary. Maybe by now, someone would have realised that they'd gone. Or had their escape been just too easy? But there was no time to consider that now. It would have to be left for later on, when they knew what the safe contained.

'No, you're right.' Nat sounded penitent. 'No time for messing about.' He walked across and chose a panel which seemed identical to all the others. Jess realised that she was holding her breath. Beside her, Sam felt for her hand.

Nat tapped in the top right-hand corner. Nothing happened.

'What's the matter?' Oliver demanded. He had sweat on his forehead. 'Has the explosion affected that too?'

'Sorry. I always forget the exact one.' Nat grinned again.

'Just get on with it.' Oliver swore at him.

'There's no need to shout,' Sam said. 'I'm sure Nat's doing his best. We all want to get this sorted out.'

Jess knew now what Nat was doing. He was trying to rattle Oliver and get him to betray his true feelings, if not worse. He *didn't* trust him. But if he

212

was right, this was a risky strategy.

Nat said, 'Here we go. It's the fourth from the left, not the fifth.' Once more, he exerted pressure — and the panel slid open, revealing the safe.

Jess stared at it, realising that until now she hadn't really believed it existed. They only had the numbers to go on. It had been a bit of a long shot, although it seemed Nat and Oliver had already known. But here it was, and now they must deal with the contents. If the numbers they had carried would unlock it . . .

She still had the paper folded tightly in her hand. Suddenly she was very calm. 'We don't know the order. We might have to have several goes. That won't upset the mechanism, will it?'

'I shouldn't think it's sophisticated enough,' Nat said. 'It's been there more than twenty years.'

'Age,' Oliver said sharply. 'Try that. Order of ages. Me, you, Sam. You do it, Jess.'

She stepped forward, looking at the

others. 'Everyone okay with that?' And, as they nodded, she bent to key in the numbers.

Nothing happened. Jess frowned. 'Can't say I'm into safes much. Should I have pressed something else?'

'Why not ask *him*?' Oliver snapped. 'He seems to be very knowledgeable. Knows a lot more than he's letting on, if you ask me.'

'Hey, be cool, mate,' Nat said. 'I only knew where it was. From now on, I don't know any more than anyone else.'

'Stop it, both of you,' Sam said. 'This isn't helping.'

'I'll try a different order,' Jess said quickly. '*Starting* with Sam.' But if Oliver was this edgy before the safe was even open, how was he going to react to their plan of returning the contents? No use worrying about that now; she was committed to opening it. 'There.' Oliver's set of numbers were keyed in.

The lock clicked, twice. Jess turned the handle and the door opened.

Inside there were three nondescript

cardboard boxes, about a foot square. This time she didn't wait for anyone's agreement. She reached in and took one out, taken aback to begin with by the weight of it. She turned and rested it on the bed. Sam and Nat were looking over her shoulders. Oliver was standing behind them, separating himself from the others.

She opened the lid. At first she didn't realise what she was looking at. The box was filled tightly with gleaming rectangular blocks. They couldn't be, could they?

'Gold,' Nat said. 'So that was it.'

'Wow,' Jess said. A mixture of emotions: awe, and a deeply saddened understanding. Everything her father had said about multiple owners and being impossible to trace such a complex amount of money had been yet another lie.

Sam said, 'It wasn't money at all. But very valuable. No wonder the gang members went to so much trouble to hide it. But it should be quite easy to identify the owner and return it.'

'Yes.' Jess was thinking, *Be practical.* If they could only return it, maybe that would exonerate her father — or partly.

'And he waited so long,' Sam was saying, 'before he managed to gather us all together.'

'Waiting for the original owner to die?' Nat suggested. 'Not just the original gang members.'

Jess thought, *Yes.* That news Lucas had brought. What was it he'd said?

'But it's not going to him, is it?' Sam said quickly. 'That's what we agreed, didn't we, Jess? We should get the police here and let them take over. This is too big for us to manage.'

'Seems the best plan,' Nat agreed. 'Safer than carrying it around Leeds, looking for a police station.'

Jess said, 'Oliver?' And froze as she turned.

A familiar voice said, 'You won't need to be carrying it anywhere. Except over here, to me.'

Leo Dryden stood in the doorway with a gun in his hand.

# 17

Sam saw her sister's face go white. Sam turned, already recognising the voice. *No, not him again.* Not now when they were going to sort it all out and put things right.

'No need for alarm,' Leo Dryden said. 'No one's going to get hurt. Just do as I say and everything will be fine.'

'No,' Jess said. The colour was returning to her face as she straightened up. 'How can it be? Look at the trouble this stuff has caused over the years. And it isn't yours.'

Leo laughed. 'And it didn't belong to the person we took it from, either — so no harm done there.'

Jess said coldly, 'You said it belonged to a number of people so it would be impossible to return it.'

'It must have done. There's such a mix in those boxes — gold, uncut diamonds, you name it. I've no idea where my source got it from, and I don't care. And neither does he, now. He died a fortnight ago. So, nobody move, and we'll be out of your way in minutes.'

'Where are you going?' Jess said.

'Don't worry, I'll be in touch. Of course I will. But I doubt if your new siblings are that bothered.' Without turning his head, he spoke to someone in the corridor behind him. 'Put the bag on the floor, Claire, and stand back here by me.'

Sam's eyes widened. She felt even more angry and confused, although doing her best to hide it. She was already furious with Nat for the pretence that had driven their relationship; she still loved him, but she couldn't forgive him that easily.

And everything her mother had hinted at, when she would turn away tight-lipped at Sam's questions about her father, had turned out to be true. He was rotten, through and through.

But he couldn't be allowed to get away with this.

And now Claire was here but with an expression of sullen anger on her face. It was too much to take in. Sam's first thought was, *Thank goodness*. Claire was her friend. That must mean everything would be all right. Mustn't it?

She said, 'Claire, I didn't know you knew my father.' She turned to Jess. 'You remember my friend, Claire.'

Jess merely looked wary. 'The one who tried to push you under a car? Oh, yes.'

Claire was coming fully into the room, placing two sports bags down on the floor. Opening them up, she said, 'She's lying, Sam. I wouldn't do that.'

Sam felt as if she was in the middle of some complicated TV drama she couldn't follow. She murmured, 'No, of course not.' But she wasn't convinced.

Claire was now standing by Leo again, turning to face him. 'Why didn't you tell me Sam was your daughter?'

she hissed. 'You've made a fool of me.'

'People work for me on a need-to-know basis,' Leo Dryden said calmly.

Sam shook her head. 'You work for him? As well as working in our office?'

'It was the same thing, once you started there. He wanted me to follow you, Sam, and report back. He didn't tell me why or who you were. I thought — well, never mind that. Anyway, I didn't need to do it in the evenings once Lucas had taken over, when you let him. You were really difficult about that.'

'And was killing her part of your brief?' Jess said angrily.

'Of course not! We were all crowded together on that traffic island, and I don't know what happened.' Claire glared at Sam as if the whole thing had been her fault.

Sam shook her head. She'd thought that in leaving home, she would achieve freedom; yet evidently she had been more observed than she had ever been in London. As far as she could tell.

How dare he? And all of them.

Leo Dryden's face was cold. 'You were jealous, you stupid fool! And presuming on what has only ever been a casual attachment.'

'No, never. I wouldn't,' Claire bleated.

'Well, never mind all that now,' Leo Dryden said irritably. 'We'll sort it out later. You can make yourself useful shortly. Jess, put as much as you can carry into one of the bags. Just you.'

Sam was trying to work out what they could do. They couldn't let this objectionable man get away with this. She had wondered and fantasised about her father for years, and now she had her wish and was regretting it. Her mother had been right all along.

His power was all in that gun he was holding. Otherwise, he was one against four. And she was almost certain he was bluffing. It was all an empty threat. He wouldn't shoot Jess. Or herself — because she was his daughter too, and he seemed to have gone to a lot of trouble to seek her out and watch out for her. If she could catch Jess's eye somehow, maybe they could risk jumping him.

And what about Claire, as she followed his instructions? Had her friendship been *all* pretence? But obviously Jess didn't trust her. Perhaps Jess could have been mistaken. No, get real. Jess didn't make mistakes.

Nat said, 'Okay.' He passed the box he was holding to Jess.

Nat. He was the one in the greatest danger. Leo Dryden would have no reluctance in shooting *him*. She swallowed. They couldn't risk it. But did Nat realise that?

She glanced at him. He was looking warily at Leo — and around him and past him. Obviously he was evaluating the risks and working something out. She hoped desperately that Leo hadn't noticed.

Sam shook her head, but Nat wasn't looking at her. As instructed, he was slowly and carefully making sure that Jess was able to take the weight of the box, slowly and carefully turning back to the safe and taking another.

Sam looked at Leo, her eyes narrowed with concentration. Almost imperceptibly, he seemed to have relaxed. He thought he'd pulled it off and success was in his grasp. No one was opposing him.

But Jess didn't turn so readily for the last one. Nat seemed to be struggling with the weight of it; he had to come halfway across the room to reach her.

Suddenly he was throwing the box directly at Leo Dryden. And at the same time, Oliver appeared behind their father and Claire, knocking Leo's arm and wresting the gun out of his hand as he stumbled.

Nat grinned. Oliver was holding the gun over Leo. 'Good teamwork.'

Sam was open mouthed. 'Oliver! Where did you come from? You were in here a minute ago.'

'You all seemed to have forgotten about our dear father here. I hadn't. I was expecting him, and I heard him coming. I saw that the en suite had an adjoining door to the landing when I was looking for the safe. Right. Get something to tie their hands, one of you.'

Leo Dryden laughed. 'This is ludicrous. What do you think you're doing, Oliver? This isn't what we planned.' He turned to address his daughters — and Jess in particular, Sam thought. 'Didn't you think you'd escaped from the cellar very conveniently?'

'Yes,' Jess said, 'as it happens.'

'All part of our strategy. Oliver and me together. He's on my side — or he said he was. So if you think he's suddenly working with you, I shouldn't count on him.'

'I'm not on anyone's side. Only my own,' Oliver said. 'There's only one person I can rely on, and that's myself. I've learned that the hard way.'

'Ah, now we're getting the poor-little-me slant,' Leo Dryden sneered. 'It's time you grew up.'

Sam suddenly saw red. 'And why shouldn't he feel that way? That's your fault too. Are you surprised, the way you treated him?'

Oliver shrugged. 'Thanks. But don't think you can win me round by pretending to stick up for me.'

'I wasn't,' Sam said indignantly. 'I meant it.'

'Yes,' Jess said. 'She does. With Sam, what you see is what you get. But I can't expect you to understand that.'

'Here,' Nat said, producing a roll of what looked like wire from a cupboard. 'Let's get on with it. No point in falling out amongst ourselves. That's what he's hoping we'll do.'

'Okay. Jess, you tie Claire,' Oliver said. 'Wrists and ankles.'

'It will be a pleasure,' Jess said. 'I don't think Sam believes, even now, what you were trying to do to her. She would be too easy on you.'

'Please don't hurt me,' Claire begged. 'It wouldn't have killed her. The traffic was only moving slowly. It was a mistake.'

'Shut up, you fool,' Leo snapped.

'That's it,' Oliver said. 'Ankles as well, and now shove her on the bed out of the way.'

Jess pushed Claire backwards and heaved her legs up.

'What are you going to do? What's going to happen to me? You're not going to leave me here?'

Oliver shrugged. 'Strangely enough I can't think of any useful purpose for you. Not even as a lever to persuade your boyfriend here to do what we want. I get the strongest impression that he's had enough of you. You're surplus to requirements.'

'Boyfriend?' Sam gasped. She felt as if her brain was spinning.

'Looks like it,' Jess said. 'I didn't know Dad had a girlfriend at present, but he's always kept his private life private.' She sounded hard and brittle, but Sam sensed her hurt.

Oliver was saying, 'Think yourself lucky, because no, we're not going to hurt you. I don't see much point in it. But explaining yourself to the police

when they find you — assuming they
do — might prove difficult. Right, Nat,
you tie Dryden. I don't trust Jess to
make a good enough job of it.'

'Oh, thanks,' Jess said.

'Divided loyalties and all that. Probably inevitable.'

Sam wished uneasily that Oliver's
instructions weren't accompanied by a
gesture from the gun. Surely they were
all on the same side in being against
their father?

'Not his feet,' Oliver said. 'He's
coming with us. Get his car keys.'

'Good idea,' Nat said. He felt in the
older man's pockets, paused as Oliver
held out his free hand for them — and
then shrugged. 'Okay, there you are.'

Oliver grinned. The first time, Sam
thought, that she had seen him smile;
but was that a good thing? She wasn't
sure. He made another casual gesture
with the gun which seemed to include
all of them. 'Okay, let's go.'

'Watch where you're pointing that,'
Nat said. 'Stick to targeting the enemy

if you don't mind.'

'No problem. I'm used to guns. Franklin was a keen gun club member. Very keen.'

Sam shivered, not liking the way he'd said that. What was he intending to do with it? And the rest? What else had his adoptive father been keen on?

Jess said, 'Glad to hear it. Where are we going?'

'You'll see. I've had an idea.'

'Care to share it with us?' Nat said, still in the same neutral tone.

'Shortly.' Oliver tilted his head, and also the gun, in Leo Dryden's direction. Presumably meaning he didn't want him to know about it, whatever it was. Which made sense, Sam thought. Oliver leaned forwards and took up the larger bag, without dropping his gaze. 'You bring the small one, Sam.'

'It's heavy,' Nat said. 'Can you manage it?'

'I'll be fine.'

Oliver grinned again. 'Let's face it, Sam's the only one we can all trust.'

Sam braced herself, but gasped at the weight all the same. 'I'm okay.'

'Come on, then. You first, Nat, then this low-life waste of space, then me — and Jess and Sam at the back. Jess last.'

Jess was glaring at him, but she fell in behind Sam without argument as they made their way down the stairs, out through the back door, and round to the front. Sam was gripping the bag with both hands, teeth gritted. There was now another car parked on the gravel drive next to Nat's. *Must be Leo's*, Sam thought.

'We'll take that one,' Oliver stated. 'Put your bag down by me and open the front passenger door, Sam.' He turned to Dryden. 'Now get in.'

'I can open the door,' Jess said. 'Sam's got enough to do.'

'You're not going near him. I don't trust him with you. Or you with him.'

'Makes sense, Jess,' Nat said, but Sam could see the wariness in his eyes. Sam put the bag down with relief, resisting the temptation to rub her wrists.

Leo Dryden moved over to the door, saying nothing. No doubt he was trying to work out what they were going to do, and how he could get out of it. He climbed in, awkwardly, with his hands tied.

Oliver said, 'Give him a shove, Nat.'

'It's all right,' Dryden said. 'I can do it, thanks.'

Sam gave Oliver a questioning look and closed the car door. 'We'll have the bags in the boot,' Oliver said.

He opened it and Nat put the bags in, turning to face Oliver. 'You can share this great idea with us now.'

Oliver considered, and shook his head. 'I don't think so. I have a feeling you might not like it.'

'So I definitely need to know it.' Nat's voice was still calm, but Sam could see the tension in his shoulders.

Jess moved towards one of the rear doors of her father's car, and suddenly the gun was pointing directly at her.

'No, you don't.'

'What? Why not? What do you think you're doing?'

'You get in Nat's car. And you, Nat.'

Nat said, 'I don't think so.'

There was a brief moment when everyone was still, before, in one swift movement, Oliver had an arm round Sam's neck and the gun to her head.

# 18

Sam screamed: a howl of fright, frustration, and annoyance at herself. Why hadn't she seen that coming? Nat would never do anything to endanger her; Oliver must have picked up on that.

'It's okay,' Oliver said. 'She won't get hurt. That's not the plan. Just as long as you two get into your car and get ready to follow us.'

Jess shouted, 'I should never have trusted you.'

'I didn't think you ever had. Why should I mean anything to you?'

Nat placed a hand on her arm. 'Come on, Jess.'

She brushed her hair back angrily, but followed his lead, and sat in the passenger seat as Nat went to the driver's side.

Nat was planning something; Sam was certain of it. If he made use of the car and suddenly drove towards Oliver, she must be ready to leap out of the way. If Oliver was taken by surprise, he wouldn't manage to shoot; just as their father had been jumped minutes before. Surely she could manage that? She tried to send Nat an encouraging look, widening her eyes and attempting a smile.

Oliver was still gripping her neck. He moved the gun from her head and levelled it at the car windscreen.

'No,' Sam shrieked, tugging at his arm as he fired. Two shots — Sam gazed in horror, expecting to see two slumped figures covered in blood and a shattered windscreen.

The windscreen was intact. Nat and Jess had both dived for cover below the dashboard.

She felt the pressure of the metal barrel against her head once more. 'Now, into this car. You're driving.'

'Driving?' Sam repeated, numb with shock. 'But what about Nat and Jess? What have you done? We have to see if they're all right.'

Oliver shook his head. 'Nothing, you idiot. They're fine. I only shot at the tyres. Get in — or they may not be. I'll be in the back, and I'll have the gun pointing at you all the time. Just remember that. But your boyfriend and your sister won't be tempted to interfere, because they won't be following us.'

Sam said, 'I can't drive.' That was true enough: she'd had one course of lessons, failed her test, and hadn't got round to taking it again. She hadn't needed to drive in London. She would probably be capable of controlling the car, but Oliver didn't know that.

He swore. 'Okay, doesn't matter. You get in the back.'

Sam obeyed. 'You can't drive and hold the gun at the same time. You don't need the gun now.'

'Very clever. But don't worry, I'll manage.' He held the steering wheel in his left hand and the gun in his right. Sam sighed. Obviously he *could* manage. Unless his impaired grip on the gun meant that she could grapple it away from him?

She dismissed that thought straight away as Oliver set off with a screeching of tyres and a punishing turn. But what was he going to do?

★ ★ ★

Jess cried out in frustration watching the silver car set off. Nat banged the flat of his hand onto the steering wheel. 'Idiot. I should have known he'd do something like that.'

'I'm sorry. I didn't know my dad had a gun.'

'Neither did I, and I've been stupid enough to let him employ me. And worse, once I fell for Sam, I should have told her what was going on, rather than tried to keep her out of danger by disappearing out of her life. I hoped I could sort things out and go back for her. Should have remembered how determined Sam can be — Okay, I know!' He shot out of the car.

'Where are you going?' Jess shot out after him. He needn't think he could disappear on *her*.

He raised a hand, obviously listening. 'Ssh.'

Jess frowned, listening with him. For what? Yes, distantly she could still hear the car and the crunch of the gears as Oliver negotiated the gateposts.

'The gear lever's always been stiff,' she muttered. And just as well, as it happened.

'They've turned right,' Nat said. 'Come on.'

'Where?' Jess followed as he jogged off, seemingly at random, into the shrubbery.

'He's turned right, and that road doesn't go anywhere. Only to the old quarry.'

And this was Quarry House, wasn't it? 'Okay,' Jess said, jogging after him.

'Shortcut,' Nat said, and didn't waste his breath on anything else.

★　★　★

Sam was anticipating a left turn out of the gateway, and her body was reacting in readiness. Oliver slammed the car sharply to the right with a squealing of brakes and gears. Sam felt dizzy as her head spun and her body struggled to adjust. They were now speeding down a little-used lane, edged with potholes, and with grass growing in the centre. Oliver's foot was hard down on the accelerator.

Leo Dryden said calmly, 'This doesn't go anywhere.'

'Oh, but it does.'

Ahead of them, Sam could see over Oliver's shoulder that the lane ended in a pair of rusted and padlocked gates. Signs reading *Danger. Keep Out.* Oliver kept going. Sam screamed, 'Stop!' She put her hands over her eyes as the car hit the gates full on, going through them as if they were cardboard.

Where were they? What was this? She screamed again. 'Please stop.'

Abruptly the car stopped. Not, she knew, in response to her fear. Oliver was laughing.

A wonder that Leo Dryden hadn't cannoned into the windscreen, as no one had fastened his seatbelt. He merely sounded bored, however. 'Right, son, you've made your gesture. Now are you going to tell us what this is all about?'

Sam was shaking. This wouldn't do. She had to hold herself together and work out how to get them all out of this, whatever Oliver was planning. *What would Jess do in this situation?* she wondered frantically. That didn't help. She didn't know.

Oliver's voice sounded almost as calm as his father's, and yet there was an underlying feverish intensity. 'You can't fool me. I know we haven't got all of it in those bags. It's all been too easy. This is only a small part, and you intended to disappear with the rest of it. Far more than your share should have been. If you were entitled to a share at all. So — you'd better tell me where it is.'

Sam stared at him. Was he having some kind of breakdown? Why come here?

Leo Dryden laughed. 'First let me go, and then I'll tell you.'

'No chance. I'm not falling for that.'

'You see, there's just no point in my telling you. I know you intend on killing me anyway. You're my son, after all. I know how you think.'

'Don't tell me I'm in any way like you.' Oliver turned to face Sam; she was shocked by the expression in his eyes. For the first time she could believe that, yes, he did intend to kill their father.

She tried to stop her voice quivering. 'Nobody needs to get hurt at all. And I think he's telling the truth and this is all there is. Besides, there's surely enough for you here. You can have it all. The others won't mind. We don't want it.'

'You don't fool anyone, Sam. I know you see yourself as the family conscience, always falling over yourself to do the right thing. But that doesn't matter. I'm taking it all anyway. It's my due after what I've been through.'

'No, you're right. You deserve something back. Just take it and leave us. We won't try to come after you.'

'That's fine, and I will — as far as it goes. But there's a small matter of retribution that has to be settled first.' His voice was grim and determined, but at least he was calm.

Leo Dryden said, 'Killing me isn't a good idea. You must know that. Shooting me here, in front of a witness? You might as well leave a calling card. Unless you intend on shooting Sam, too? As well as Nat and Jess?'

Sam let out a squeal of fright. 'No, please.'

'Don't worry, Sam. He won't. He hasn't got the bottle.'

What on earth was her father doing? Oliver's moods seemed to alter at the speed of lightning as it was. Perhaps Leo Dryden was trying to rattle him into making mistakes. A very dangerous game, if so.

Oliver snarled. 'And you'd know all about that, wouldn't you? I know who was behind the supposed gas explosion that killed Nat's parents.'

Leo Dryden's voice was quiet and deadly. 'I didn't kill them, and you know it. None better. I may have thought about it, but in the end, I didn't need to. It was you.'

Sam gasped, her hands to her mouth. Surely Oliver wasn't capable of murder, in spite of his miserable and probably abusive childhood?

'And so what if I did? You think you're invincible, don't you? You're not. And you fully deserve what's coming to you. Just like Franklin did.' His voice rose, and the gun was only inches from Leo Dryden's head. 'But you haven't succeeded in distracting me. First, you're going to tell me about the rest of it. Like I said.'

Dryden said wearily, 'There is no more.' He sounded bored.

'Of course there is. There isn't enough here to warrant taking the risks you took, or ruining so many lives over so many years.' Without turning his head, Oliver said, 'Get out of the car, Sam.'

241

Sam stared at him. There wasn't much doubt now about the danger her father was in. And no one deserved to die like this, whatever they might have done.

She took a deep breath. 'No. You'll have to kill me too.'

'What?' Oliver turned to face her, obviously taken aback. 'Ah, I get it. But what makes you think I wouldn't? Why should I care about you? You and Jess had everything between you. I had worse than nothing.'

Dryden said, 'That wasn't her fault.'

His attention diverted, Oliver swung the gun back to him. He was raging now at the opposition to his plan, his face dark. Sam had thought he'd been dangerous before, but now he would be lethal. He was no longer thinking coolly and clearly.

But *she* was. If they were to get out of here without any further harm, it was down to her. She had to stop him. Quietly, and without looking down, she moved her feet from side to side, hoping to find something to help her. Nothing. What about the pocket on the back of the seat in front of her? She could tell there was something inside it. More risky, though. Would Oliver be able to tell that she was looking for it?

Leo Dryden was still working on his strategy of provocation. She wished he wouldn't. He was saying, 'You were happy enough to work with me when it suited you.' At least this was distracting Oliver from Sam's movements. Yes. There *was* something, smooth and cylindrical. A heavy, substantial torch.

Her father said, 'You went along with me when I needed you to go along with the pretence of kidnapping Jess.'

'What?' Sam cried, unable to help herself, almost dropping the torch and ruining the whole thing. She forgot about not drawing attention to herself. 'But Oliver, why? Whyever would you do that? We trusted you.'

He turned back to her as she resisted the temptation to look down at the torch on her knees. 'I helped both of you to gain your confidence, obviously. So that we could eventually discover where the gold heist was.'

'No, I mean, why kidnap Jess at all?'

Oliver laughed harshly. 'Ask him. His plan.'

Leo Dryden smiled. She wondered how he could, in this situation. You had to admire his courage, she supposed. 'To protect her. I didn't want her to get involved any further. And I tried to protect you as well, Sam. But neither of you would keep out of it. Difficult, like your mother. Oliver gained Jess's trust by rescuing her, as planned, and was then instructed to protect her.'

Sam frowned. It didn't quite make sense. Partly right, no doubt but not entirely. But was that important? It was obvious she couldn't trust either of them. That was what mattered.

Leo Dryden was nodding, as if at his own cleverness. 'Oliver was watching over Jess and Lucas was doing the same for you, Sam. After Nat let me down, not being man enough to follow the task through. But I can't say any of you made a very good job of it.'

Oliver said, 'Oh, I think I did all right. I've got you where I want you now.'

'Have you, though? You don't think you have all of the stuff, do you? You were right. The rest of it is mostly diamonds, if I recall correctly. Easier to hide, easy to carry. You have some, of course, but not all.'

Oliver shouted, 'Shut up!' He leaned back, pointing the gun at his father's head.

Sam thought, *Now. It has to be now.* She raised the torch with both hands, closed her eyes and brought it down on the back of Oliver's skull with all her strength.

Leo shouted, 'Good girl!' Somehow, his hands were free. He knocked the gun upwards as Oliver slumped across the dashboard.

The car shuddered and jerked forwards. Sam thought, quite calmly, that Oliver's foot must have been resting on the brake pedal. As if in slow motion, the car slid over the lip of the rocks in front of them, toppled, and fell.

* * *

Jess had never run so fast in her life. Ahead of them, they could still hear the car engine. They came through the splintered and smashed gate. Her heart was thumping in her ribcage, and her legs felt as if they would give way. But it was not fast enough.

They were only just in time to see the car disappear over the edge. Jess screamed, 'No!' Listening for the inevitable crash from below as the car hit the bottom of the quarry. It didn't come.

Nat reached the edge of the slabs of rock only one pace ahead of her. He peered down, his face white. Jess took a deep breath and looked over too.

The car was caught on a jutting ledge, held only by a young and slender rowan sapling. She let out a long sigh of relief. But no one inside seemed to be moving. Just as well, as probably the slightest alteration of balance could send it into the drop below.

She said, 'We have to get them out. Sam first.'

'Yes. I'll put my weight onto the boot, and you see if you can open the back door.'

They moved quickly but cautiously down the steep slope; gripping onto the rocks, small shrubs, anything there was.

Nat said, 'Strictly speaking, we should get them out of the front seats first. For the balance.'

Jess didn't pause. 'No. Sam first.'

He murmured, 'Thanks.'

So he did care. Jess thought, *We haven't done it yet. Two steps more, one . . .* She could reach the door handle. Hardly breathing at all, she pressed it gently.

Nat said, 'I've put a couple of stones behind this wheel.'

'Okay.' She felt his weight as he leaned down on the boot, giving a momentary stability. Mustn't let the door swing open.

That would wreck the whole thing. *A delicate balance.* She found she was muttering those words to herself like some kind of mantra. 'Sam? Are you all right? Can you hear me? We're going to get you out.' *Delicate balance.* 'Only move very, very slowly. An inch at a time. It's a delicate balance.'

Sam turned to face her. She glanced down at the quarry below them and gulped. 'Yes. I can do it.'

'Take my hand. I'm holding the door.' In the passenger seat, her father moved his head. 'Dad? Are you okay? We'll help you in a minute.' She hoped and prayed that was true. *Don't think about it.*

'Just get your sister out, Jess. Don't worry about me.'

Nat said, 'The gold's heavy, don't forget. That's helping.'

Yes, of course it was. Sam was edging along the seat, taking the hand Jess stretched out to her. If it went now, the door would take both of them. *Don't think about it.* 'Put one foot out, Sam.'

She felt the car sway slightly, but said nothing. If Sam panicked, she might move too quickly. One foot out, both hands clasped in hers, and then the other foot — edging round the obstacle of the door — and Sam was out, both sisters swaying together.

# 19

They clung to each other for no more than a few seconds before Jess leaned back carefully on the support of the sloping rock. She said, 'Go back up to the top where you'll be safe. I'm going to get Dad out.'

'No way,' Sam said. 'I'll lean on the boot with Nat.'

'Thanks.' Jess began to make her way round the back of the car. Sam was slender, but there was no doubt that her weight would make a difference.

Nat said, 'Just open the door for him. Don't hang around, Jess. It could take you with it.'

Jess ignored him. 'Dad?' Slowly and gently, she opened the door and leaned inside.

'I'll be fine. It's okay. I got my hands free without him noticing.' He nodded towards Oliver, who was slumped over the wheel. 'You just make sure the door doesn't swing, Jess.'

She called past him. 'Oliver? Don't move. We'll be round for you in a minute.'

'He can't hear you,' Leo Dryden said. 'He's unconscious.'

'I hit him on the head,' Sam said, her voice quivering. 'Is he still breathing?'

'Don't worry, Sam. He'll be fine.' Their father sounded convincing.

Jess said nothing. He didn't look too good to her. Two of them would have to pull him out. He wouldn't be able to help them. But one person at a time. 'I've got the door, Dad.'

He smiled at her. 'Good girl. That's great.' As if everything was normal and ordinary. As if none of this had ever happened.

Jess stretched out her right hand so he didn't need to jerk himself from the seat. All fine. He was edging out smoothly, just as Sam had done. Nearly. He smiled at her and glanced upwards.

And stopped. The colour drained from his face.

Nat was saying, 'Don't worry, Jess. We've got it. And the gold is fairly heavy on its own.'

A voice from above and behind them said, 'Stop there. That gold is mine and I'm taking it now.'

Her first feeling was of profound and weakening relief. Help was here. They would be all right.

Or would they? A great many things came together in Jess's head, all at once. She was beginning to understand. For once, her father had been telling the truth. There had indeed been someone, greater than him in wealth and power, calling the shots. And what else?

Her father said, his voice strained, 'Smithson Pike! But you're dead.'

'Exactly what I wanted you to think, Leo. Not difficult to send you the news you wanted via a trusted messenger, backing that up with fake obituaries in the media and a memorial page on Facebook. Unfortunately for you, you fell for it. That's why I'm where I am, in a very comfortable position, whereas you've spent twenty years running and hiding from me. But you didn't even succeed in that. Thinking a change of name and address would be enough? So very, very mistaken.'

Everything about her father seemed to have altered. He was suddenly aged, shrunken inside himself, with the arrogant confidence lost. He threw his arms upwards in a gesture of hopeless defeat. The car rocked, and the rowan bent and settled again.

'No,' Jess said. 'You can't give up. I'm getting you out.' Whatever this man had on him, it wasn't worth a life. And although she couldn't see the new-comer too well from down here, he didn't seem that frightening. His voice was strong, but he was frail and bent, leaning heavily on a stick.

'Quite right,' the voice said. 'Listen to your daughter.' He turned his head. Two other figures, both wearing black, were standing on either side of him. As he snapped his fingers, they began to lower themselves down the slope. One took the boot, adding his weight. The other was down beside Jess now, taking her father's arms. Their boss might be frail, but they were strong and solid.

The one next to her pushed her aside; and even without that, the way he seized hold of her father was setting alarm bells ringing.

The voice above said, 'Don't even think of jumping, Leo. Far too quick and easy. I've got a much better idea.'

As her father was pulled past her, Jess hissed, 'Who is this?'

Her father's eyes were haunted. 'You don't need to know. Please, Jess. Keep out of it this time.'

'Wise advice, Jess.'

Jess blinked up at him. This Smithson Pike had the manpower, and he was in control of the situation. Yes, even without her father's warning, she could accept now that he was dangerous.

Pike said, 'And now we'll have my property out of that boot.' He nodded to his man.

Jess said, 'But what about Oliver? We

have to get him out. Without the bags, the car will overbalance.'

'There's no *have to*. He's probably dead already. Agreed?'

The man holding Leo nodded. 'Looked dead to me, Boss.'

Sam whimpered.

'Why should he be?' Jess cried. 'Of course he isn't. Sam can't have hit him that hard. We can't just leave him.'

'Why not? He's always maintained that he's been *surplus to requirements*. You see, I pride myself on keeping up with what's going on. That being so, why try to contradict Oliver's view of himself now? And why should you care? He's betrayed you, lied to you — '

'He's our brother.'

He laughed. 'You've only just discovered that he exists. You'd both very conveniently forgotten about him. Enough. This is boring me. Open the boot.'

Jess wanted desperately to stop them, but couldn't see how. Already the two bags were being hefted out, as if they weighed nothing. Once this man had left, they would be even more powerless to help her father. And he would be in grave danger.

Perhaps she could delay him. If she could keep Pike talking, maybe Nat or Sam might be able to ring 999. Worth a try — but she didn't dare look at either of them to try and communicate what she wanted them to do.

'How is this stuff yours, anyway? Is it the proceeds of some huge robbery? It seems an odd mix.'

'So you've looked at it?' A disturbing note in his voice. 'Nothing to lose by telling you, in that case. After all, your father is equally culpable. Try to inform anyone about me and you inevitably involve him, so if I were you I shouldn't try that. Yes, this is the proceeds of various robberies, performed when your father worked for me. But his success gave him the mistaken idea that all this should belong to him. He worked out a way of having it for himself, along with the happy little band he persuaded into assisting him. Subcontractors, you might say. Although whether they were ever intended to receive a share, I would sincerely doubt. He persuaded them into concealing my property until the heat had died down. That's what you told them, wasn't it, Leo? Oddly enough, none of them survived long enough to achieve this aim. All the more for the one who did survive. How fortuitous.'

With a brief return of his old self, Leo Dryden said, 'You had plenty. I thought you'd hardly miss it.'

'Unfortunately for you, I did miss it. And now I am reclaiming what is mine. Learn this, Leo: I always do. Enough. Time to go.' He grinned as Leo Dryden was manhandled to the top of the slope. 'Say your goodbyes — but you'll have to be quick.' Another man appeared behind him, hanging back a little.

So there were at least three of them, Jess thought. Her father was making no attempt to struggle, or even to say goodbye as suggested. He stumbled as he was led away. Jess felt numb, powerless. They were gone. She could no longer hear their voices or footsteps.

She thought, *We have to stop them*. She couldn't just let them take him away. What was going to happen to him? No consolation in knowing he'd brought all this on himself and most people would think he deserved his fate, whatever it might be. Better by far if they had been able to hand him over to the police.

With only Nat and Sam to hold it, the car had been swaying gently on the edge. Now, suddenly, the roots of the rowan came away from the cliff. Almost gracefully, the car slid forwards — and then toppled abruptly downwards, bouncing and turning as it fell.

Jess felt as if she didn't know which way to turn. She could hardly think straight, pulled in every direction at once. Like a switch inside her head, her thoughts cleared, and she lowered herself to join Sam and Nat as they peered down into the quarry.

'What about Oliver?' Sam said. 'Do you think he's all right? We have to go and see.'

'We can't get down there,' Nat said. 'And couldn't do much for him if we did. We haven't got the equipment.' He took out his phone. 'I'll ring 999 and let the emergency services deal with it. It's the best we can do.'

'And my father?' Jess whispered, feeling that she hardly dared ask.

Nat finished the call, and paused as if considering what she had said.

Sam said, 'We have to do something for him.'

Nat said, 'Do we?'

Sam put a hand on his arm. 'He didn't kill your parents, Nat. It was Oliver. He admitted it when I was in the car. We can't just let them take him. Shall we ring the police and report an abduction?'

Nat exhaled, slowly. 'I see. Yes, that makes sense. Well, there's no point in phoning the police. What would we tell them? We don't even know what kind of car Pike came in, let alone the registration. Okay.' He came to a decision. 'I do think we should get out of here. First of all, we have to get ourselves mobile again — ready for when we *have* formed some kind of plan.'

'Oliver shot the front tyres,' Sam said. 'Both of them.'

'Yes, but I've a spare in the car and another in the garage. Not too wonderful, that one, but it will do. And while we're seeing to that, we'll be out of the way of the rescue services. We don't need to get tangled up in making statements, and they won't need us.'

That was true. They weren't even needed for giving directions. The car had left a broad track of destruction from the gates, easily visible over flattened and broken saplings and shrubs.

They jogged back through the garden. Jess knew how grateful she should be to the other two. Considering how Nat's parents had suffered, she would have understood if he had chosen to leave Leo to his fate. And Sam had grown up hearing only her mother's hostile opinion of him.

This was a start. If only, between

them, they could come up with this miraculous *something*. She said, 'I can change one of the tyres while you do the other. That will be quicker.'

Nat nodded. 'Good.'

Yes, great, Jess thought. They would have a functioning vehicle. And then what? If only they could communicate with her father somehow and find out where he was. Her thoughts were spinning wildly as she began on the spare from Nat's boot, while Nat ran over to the garage.

Sam said suddenly, 'Did you see that third man, the one at the top? We never got a good look at him. He kept his head down. But I know now. It was Lucas.'

'Lucas?'

'My ex-boyfriend,' Sam said calmly. 'I'll text him.'

What? What on earth was Sam doing? Jess knew who she meant, she couldn't forget that spark of electricity she'd felt when he'd come to the house in Leeds. Quite ridiculous. Like some lovestruck teen. She didn't even know him. And he'd been coming away from the park café too. Now, if Sam was right, he must be working for this powerful criminal type. Just showed. You shouldn't trust random sparks that came to you against all logic and reason.

She said, while her hands worked at unscrewing the bolts, 'What are you going to say?'

Sam read it out. '*Surprised to see you. We need help. Where are you now?*' She looked up. 'How about that?'

'Yes, fine.' Jess nodded. 'But what is he doing? He's working for this person who's got my dad.' Was making contact with him a good idea? But Sam seemed confident enough. And what else did they have?

'Who knows?' Sam said. 'That's what I'd like to find out too. Perhaps his reply will tell us which side he's on.'

Jess frowned, removing the damaged tyre, slotting the new one into position. Beginning to tighten the bolts. 'He's taking his time.'

'Depends whether Mr Powerful can see what Lucas is doing, doesn't it? Or perhaps now he knows I've sussed him, he'll just ignore me.'

Jess said, 'I thought you said he was working for my dad.'

'Yes, he was. Like Nat. Yet another person charged with looking after me, as if I couldn't look after myself.' Her phone bleeped. 'Ah, here we are.' Sam paused.

Jess said urgently, 'Does he say what he's doing? Why he's with Smithson Pike?' No, of course not. Sam hadn't asked him that. Those issues would have to wait.

By now, Nat was back and already removing the tyre on the driver's side. Sam said, 'Oh, I get it. He's sent us a postcode.'

'Is that all?'

'Probably all he could manage to send without arousing suspicion.' Sam said cheerfully, 'At least it shows he's on *our* side.'

Did it? Jess was doubtful. He could be leading them into a trap. Perhaps Smithson Pike was regretting allowing them to go so easily.

'What's this, then?' Nat asked without pausing in removing and replacing the tyre and the bolts.

Sam explained. 'I've texted Lucas — he was the man above and behind us at the quarry — and he's sent me a postcode. That's going to be really helpful, isn't it?'

Nat didn't seem to share her enthusiasm. 'Okay. That's good as far as it goes. But whose side is he on?' He stood up, wiping his hands.

Sam gave him a very direct look. 'Why ask me? Nobody I know seems to be who I thought they were.'

He grimaced. 'I asked for that. Come on, let's follow it up. I'll put the postcode into the satnav.'

Jess sat in the back, since Sam was the one in contact with their supposed guide. 'Is it far?' she was asking as Nat keyed it in.

'Same side of Leeds as we are. Not too far at all.'

Jess raised her eyebrows. 'Very nice indeed, if that's where this man lives. Or works, maybe.'

'Or maybe we're just having a trip out to the Country Forest Park.'

Jess thought, without voicing her dread, *Somewhere quiet*. Perhaps somewhere you could easily dispose of someone without being seen. She shivered. *No, snap out of it*. That wasn't going to happen because they were going to get there in time. An annoying little voice inside her head murmured, *He could be dead already*. Getting back from the quarry, changing the tyres — that had all taken far too long.

They turned left out of the gates, taking the bends far too fast for safety, but gaining the main road without any mishaps. As they blended in with the flow of traffic, a police car came from the opposite direction, siren whining and lights flashing.

'Made it,' Nat said. 'Now they can't

tell we were there. Any nearer, and they might have been pulling us in and asking what we'd seen. If not now, certainly later.'

'But eventually they'll come round and do a house-to-house, won't they?' Sam said.

'I would think so.'

'What will you say?' Jess asked.

Nat glanced over his shoulder at her. 'Haven't decided yet. That's something we'll all have to discuss later. First things first.'

# 20

Sam held her phone, aware that she must seem calm, confident, and in control of the situation, with all these sensible and helpful suggestions. Both Jess and Nat had nodded their agreement.

Inside her head, however, there was nothing but a whirling fog. She felt very confused. Yes, of course, if their father was in danger they should try to help him. But if they hadn't been able to prevent him being taken in the first place, what could they usefully do?

And surely he should be punished for his past misdeeds — which were many, by the sound of it — whether by the law or some other agency. Maybe he had only gained a kind of dark justice. No, that was a horrible thing to be thinking. Being lawfully imprisoned was one thing, but whatever was happening to him now, it certainly wasn't lawful — or controlled.

Worse — she didn't feel as if she was helping someone close to her. She had really tried over the past hours but she couldn't relate to him as a father. She had done her best to seem warm and welcoming to begin with, hoping that might trigger genuine feelings within her, but it hadn't worked. He was still a stranger.

*No,* she told herself. *Stop being stupid, asking yourself why you're doing this when it's obvious. You're doing it for Jess.* Because straight away she had felt close to Jess as a sister, as if she had known her for years. And Jess, beneath the tough and capable exterior, was distraught, Sam could tell.

She glanced sideways at Nat. And all this was before she even started on her feelings for *him*. His seeming betrayal had knocked her hard. Now she was thinking about it again, however, things were getting clearer. If he loved her, as she was still certain he did, of course he would be doing his best to help and protect her. And she'd been angry, thinking he was treating her as some kind of fragile princess who wasn't able to do anything useful. But now he was taking her seriously.

Obviously, she had witnessed a different side of Nat altogether arising from their circumstances: he had been cool, calm, and self-contained in a succession of dangerous situations, but bringing her into the events whenever appropriate, and when there had been something useful she could do to help.

She said, 'What are we going to do when we get there?'

Nat pursed his lips. 'That rather depends on Lucas.' He grinned. 'Do you trust him?'

'You mean, this may be a trap?'

Behind her, Jess said, 'Exactly. But if we're ready for that and aware — '

'Yes,' Nat said. 'Something we have to think about.'

Sam hesitated. 'I don't think it is. But Lucas isn't quite who I thought he was, obviously. Twice over, in fact. I must be really dense. Though I thought it was odd when he dumped me without warning — and then appeared here saying he wanted to start again. I'm thinking that our father must have recruited him in the first place.' She swallowed. 'Hopefully when he was already going out with me. Not good for the self-confidence if he only dated me from the start because he was being paid to. And then — he must have changed his mind. Perhaps he started working for this Smithson Pike? Who sent him back as some kind of double agent, to pretend to be working for Leo Dryden again, for his own purposes?' She paused, uncertain. 'Does all that make sense?'

'After a fashion,' Nat said, 'being guilty of something similar myself. Though I'm nothing to do with this new man, thankfully. Or any kind of criminal activity. Anyway, we're here.'

The satnav was directing them down a short track.

*Where would this man live?* Sam thought. *In a smart, detached mansion with a swimming pool and gold taps?* The track opened out onto a grassy area fronting a single-storey stone cottage, with peeling window frames and two slates missing. Not at all what she had expected.

Parked to one side stood an elderly blue Ford. That wasn't what she would have expected, either. While she stared at it, the driver's door opened, and Lucas got out.

Sam opened her door.

'If this is a trap,' Nat muttered, 'we've just driven right into it. Sorry. I'll speak to him first, and if anything happens to me, get into the driving seat and just go. I'll leave you the keys, Jess.'

'We're not leaving you here,' Sam said firmly. 'And I'm the one who knows him. He'll expect to speak to me.'

He nodded, reluctantly. 'I'll be watching your back.'

'That's fine. Thanks.' Sam walked

over to the other car, her feet feeling heavy. Lucas was watching her silently, without moving.

She said, again, 'Thanks.'

'That's okay.' Lucas seemed cautious too.

Sam thought, *Go for it*. Why not? No more messing about. 'Nat thinks you may have led us into a trap. Where's your employer — the real one?'

'No trap. Not by me. But listen, because we don't have much time.'

Behind them, there was a flurry of movement as Jess shouted, 'Where is he? What have you done with him?'

Lucas called, 'It's okay. My employer has told me to deal with Leo and deliver him here. But I haven't *dealt* with him yet, not totally.'

'Deliver him?' Sam asked. 'Who to?' She looked round. There was no one else there.

'Knock on the door of the cottage and find out. And Jess, he's in the boot. It isn't locked. And I warn you, he looks a mess, but he's alive. Come on, Sam.'

Here was the old self-confident Lucas grin. 'It's okay.'

Sam could hear Jess opening the boot as she knocked. Heard Jess exclaim, 'Dad, can you hear me?' And to Nat, 'We have to get him out.'

Lucas turned. 'No, wait. It's not that simple. Don't worry, we'll sort it, but don't get him out. Not yet.'

Sam thought, *And you think Jess will take any notice of that?* But then she heard footsteps inside the cottage and turned back to the door. As it opened, her eyes widened in astonishment. 'Mum!'

Carolyn Dryden looked equally shocked. 'Sam, you're all right! But why are *you* here?'

They flung their arms round each other. Carolyn said, the words pouring out, 'I'm so sorry, I didn't know. I was horrified when I discovered Leo was living in Leeds, but I thought at least Lucas could look after you and that Smithson would get to your father before he could do you any harm.'

Sam shook her head. 'Don't worry.

I'm fine.' Although she had no idea what her mother was talking about.

'Okay,' Lucas said. 'Hi, Carolyn. Sorry to break this up. One delivery, as arranged. That's what I've been instructed to say. And we'd better deal with that first.'

Carolyn Dryden was the first of the two to pull herself together and stand back. Hardly surprising, Sam thought, since she would have more of an idea what was going on. 'You're right. And yes, we had.'

'My boss will be getting impatient for the proof.'

Behind them, Jess said, 'What proof?'

Sam turned to smile at her, face glowing with delight. 'This is my mum — and yours too, obviously.' But there was a guarded look within Jess's eyes and no answering smile. Of course, she would feel just the same as Sam did about Leo. Defensive, cautious.

Nat said, 'What did you mean, as arranged? And proof of what, exactly?'

'First, Pike was to supervise, in

person, a further brief interrogation. That's been done and the results are all too visible, I'm afraid. Then I was instructed to bring Leo Dryden over here, to Carolyn.' His face was impassive. 'And, as a reward for her loyalty and devotion, she can either finish him off herself or watch me doing it.' His voice was steady and cold. 'After which, we dispose of the body by setting fire to the car.'

Sam's eyes were wide. Loyalty and devotion? What did he mean?

'You're not going to!' Jess was almost spitting with fury, like a wildcat, claws clenched.

'No, of course not,' Carolyn said. 'But I can't allow Leo Dryden to get away with what he's done, to me and my family. He'll get what's coming to him, and when he's arrested, I'll be first in the queue to give evidence against him.'

Lucas said quickly, 'But we have to make my boss think his instructions have been followed. I have to film it all on my phone and send it to him. Otherwise he'll be round here with reinforcements, and we'll be back to square one.'

'You mean, you're going to fake it somehow?' Sam asked, hoping desperately that *was* what Lucas meant. 'Will he believe it?'

'Fortunately for us, he's incredibly arrogant. Gets a blind spot for what people will do for him; and, because he pays well, generally they do. It won't occur to him that Carolyn or I would do anything else. That's what I'm counting on.' He turned back to the car. 'Let's get on with it. Open the boot as wide as it will go, Jess.'

Sam could read the doubt in her sister's face. Could they trust him? He could just as easily be intending to kill their father in front of them. Now he was taking a baseball bat from the rear seat. He raised his eyebrows, passing it to Carolyn. 'Your call, if you want.'

Carolyn stepped back, closed fists clasped to her chest. 'I hate him. I've hated him for years, and I lost two of my children because of him. But I can't do it.' She said bitterly, 'I'm surprised your boss thought I could. He doesn't know me at all.'

Sam frowned. Why should that man know her mother? What had been going on?

'No problem,' Lucas said. 'I'll do it. You can react however seems natural, Carolyn; because I warn you, I'm going to make it convincing. But the rest of you, step back well out of sight and keep quiet.'

He leaned over the boot and seemed to be muttering to the man inside. The gist of his words carried on the breeze. 'Don't move. I'm not going to hurt you, but it's imperative that you keep still. One hundred per cent. Okay?' He was handing Carolyn his phone. 'You hold this. It's ringing now. As soon as Pike picks up, he'll be able to see and hear everything.'

Sam moved over to Jess and took her hand, giving her a wobbly smile and mouthing, 'It's okay.' Jess nodded but she didn't seem reassured.

Lucas faced the camera, holding the bat up and giving a thumbs-up with the other hand. He turned and leaned over the boot again. Sam couldn't see the condition of the man inside, and didn't want to. But if Lucas had been talking to him, he must be conscious at least. Had she heard a grunted reply, or only imagined it?

Lucas didn't seem to be in any hurry now. 'Okay, Carolyn, here we go. This is what you've wanted for twenty years.' He grinned, giving every impression that he was enjoying himself as he raised the bat.

Sam shut her eyes, but not looking was worse. She opened them again as the bat descended into the boot; and jumped, startled, as Dryden responded with a shout of pain. Oh, no. Had it gone horribly wrong? Had Lucas missed? Next to her, Jess was stiff with tension. She must be aching to run forward and help him, Sam thought.

Lucas called, 'It's done, Carolyn. Come and look.'

Carolyn walked slowly forwards, holding the phone stretched out in front of her as if afraid of it. Considering who was on the receiving end, Sam was hardly surprised. Her mother looked down into the boot and put her free hand, fisted, into her mouth. She said, 'How odd. I don't feel anything. Now he's actually dead.' She spoke into the phone. 'Thanks. I'm very grateful.'

Lucas raised his voice. 'Get back now, Carolyn. I'm going to fire the car.'

Sam thought, *What?* How could he do that and film it? Jess pulled her arm. Obviously the warning was for the other three onlookers also. They moved away. *How far would be safe?* Sam thought wildly.

Carolyn, moving backwards, seemed to trip over a fallen branch and dropped the phone. At once, Nat ran forwards, and he and Lucas heaved and manhandled Leo Dryden out of the boot.

Sam couldn't stop herself; she glanced at his face, bruised and covered in blood. They were pulling him along, arms around his shoulders, as if he had no strength in his legs. Into the trees.

Lucas waved to Carolyn and she picked the phone up again. 'Sorry, love. Sorry, Lucas. It just slipped out of my hand. But I haven't missed anything.'

The car exploded into a ball of fire. Carolyn kept on filming for a minute or so as the heat of the flames was joined by a series of small explosions like a firework display. At last, Lucas reached for the phone, speaking loudly, one arm still raised, conveying the need for silence. 'There you go, Boss. All done. I'll be round to make my report in person.' He dropped his arm. 'Right, conversation over and film sent off. We can talk again now.'

'We need an ambulance,' Jess said. Her phone was in her hand already. 'The car will burn itself out, won't it? I won't bother with a fire engine.'

*Besides*, Sam thought, *that could still*

*be busy in the quarry with Oliver*. She shivered. 'Is he still conscious?'

Nat was kneeling beside him. 'No. Heaving him out of the boot like that was too much for him, I would think. But he's still breathing.'

'The ambulance is on its way,' Jess said. She knelt too. 'Can you hear me, Dad? The ambulance is coming. You'll be fine.'

Sam breathed a sigh of relief. No, there wasn't time for that yet. Surely they shouldn't be hanging about round here? Smithson Pike might send some of the others to check. He might hear the ambulance siren. She was suddenly feeling very vulnerable.

'How far to the house?' she asked Lucas.

'No distance. This cottage is literally at the bottom of his garden. Handy for loving visits.'

'*What?*' Sam said.

He saw the look of distaste on her face. 'Sorry. Big garden, though. Right, I'll go and make my report and you can beat a retreat if you want.'

She put a hand on his arm. 'Wait a minute. Why are you helping us if you're working for him?' There hadn't been time to ask before. There had been too much to do. 'And what if he finds out?'

He shrugged. 'All good things come to an end. And fortunately, some that aren't so good. I'll have to come clean now, and that's what I planned. I'm with the police. Working undercover.'

'What?' Sam stared at him. 'You *are* a policeman? I know you said something about it — but I didn't believe you.'

Lucas grinned. 'You weren't meant to. It was a double bluff. Not a policeman in the usual way: I'm a member of a special unit. So, I'm going back to make my report to Smithson Pike now, as I told him. He won't suspect anything. But when this job is all sewn up, that's it. I'm coming out of this line of work.'

'Right,' Sam said faintly. She felt as if she was seeing him as a different person altogether, adding on to what she had already discovered about him today.

Nat had left Leo to Jess, and was walking over, listening intently.

Lucas said, 'First I have to deal with Pike. He may have left you behind at the quarry but don't be deceived by that. He won't have forgotten about you. You three are still in a dangerous situation.'

Nat said, 'You can't tackle him on your own. You'll need help. You're in danger too.'

'I'm fine, mate. I'm used to this. Been doing it for years.'

'Don't be a fool. How are you intending to deal with him, specifically?'

Lucas gave him a considering look. 'Okay. Now he thinks Leo Dryden is dead, his major preoccupation will be the goods — which *are* identifiable, whatever he thinks. When I have him picked up by my unit, he *must* have them in his possession. He's always avoided it before.'

'Can the local force handle that?'

Lucas laughed. 'No way. The necessary armed teams are standing by, waiting for my call. We've come very near a time or two but he's managed to wriggle out of it. Disposing of the goods just before the team arrived, for instance. That's why it's important to have it all cut and dried this time, with filmed evidence.'

'He admitted it,' Sam said, 'at the quarry.'

'I know, and I switched my phone on; but the sound quality was very poor, so I doubt whether it will stand. That's why I'm going back now, as arranged, and I intend to get him talking.'

Would he fall for that? Sam thought it all sounded too easy.

'Not on your own,' Nat said obstinately. 'What about his private army? How many are there?'

'You forget, they know me and trust me too.'

'They won't be standing back while you start recording.'

'They won't be there. He doesn't trust anyone to watch him when he's going over his goods. It's a first that *I'm* going to be near at hand.' He paused, and then obviously came to a decision. 'Okay, there is something you can do.'

'And that is?'

'Like I said, he doesn't allow anyone to witness him gloating over his ill-gotten gains. But I've managed to work myself into a privileged position. Made myself different. Most of the others are employed for strength and brawn rather than any appreciation of the finer things in life. So he's allowed me to see one or two of his achievements — but small ones, not carrying much of a penalty. So I didn't go for collecting concrete evidence on them. But this one is worth the effort.'

'And where do I come in?'

'We,' Sam said firmly. 'I'm coming too.'

Only Jess, now standing beside her, seemed to have heard. 'Too right.'

Lucas was saying, 'He'll have sent the

others off to sit in the staffroom he's kindly provided for all of us. Mostly to be used when he wants us out of the way. Once there, I was hoping they'd stay put — and that he wouldn't try to contact them. But you can lock them in; far better than leaving it to chance.'

Jess said, 'It all sounds good — but is he going to stand in front of you, happily posing for the photo? *Here are some I stole earlier.* Get real. You need someone with you to take the pictures. Maybe out of sight somewhere.'

'And you're applying?' Lucas said.

'Of course. I can conceal myself somehow. I can certainly get the sound, if not much of a picture — though I will if I can. Through a window, maybe. Behind curtains. All you need to do is get him talking.'

'It's too dangerous for any of you,' Carolyn said. '*I'll* come with you, Lucas. He trusts me too.'

Jess glared at her. What was this woman doing here at all? They didn't need *her* butting in.

'Why?' Sam said suddenly. 'Why should he trust you?' She didn't want to hear the answer, but knew she had to. Was this what Lucas had been hinting at a few minutes ago?

Lucas said quickly, 'Because your mother has sacrificed herself for the greater good by having an affair with him.'

Carolyn was still looking uncomfortable. 'It was the only way.'

'To be revenged on my father?' Jess said sharply. 'By giving this criminal all the information on my father that you had?'

'Yes.'

'She couldn't just leave him to benefit from his criminal acts, could she?' Sam said. 'Or to benefit from what he'd stolen. We agreed on that, didn't we?'

'Anyway,' Carolyn said firmly, 'I can't stay here. Eventually, Smithson Pike will send someone else to check on the car — or even come down himself. Much as he likes you, Lucas, he won't leave something this important without further verification. And if he discovers we've sent for an ambulance for someone who isn't yet dead, he won't be too happy. I have to come with you.'

Sam said, 'Come with *us*. Because it's no use objecting, Nat; I can't stay here either. That's obvious. We'll have to take the car and drive round by the road, won't we? You'll be able to direct us, Mum — and tell us where best to park so the car won't be seen.'

Nat nodded. 'Good idea. That will save us a lot of time. And could even prevent us making a dangerous mistake.'

Sam smiled. 'It's great to have you here, Mum. And to know you're safe. I was worried about you, when you just took off without telling me where you were going.' She thought she understood something else, too: when her mum had been supposedly travelling for work, had she been here with Smithson Pike?

Her mother smiled back. 'No need.'

She looked over to Lucas; Sam thought it still seemed as if she was going to push for taking the part Jess had earmarked for herself.

Lucas obviously thought so too. He said quickly, 'So that's settled, then.'

# 21

Jess was glaring at Carolyn. Good. Lucas had sorted the woman out before she could object and hold things up. A pain that she had to be here at all, and Jess certainly didn't feel like working with her. Not yet, and maybe not ever. So, according to her, to be avenged on her husband, she'd got involved with somebody ten times worse? Great.

And if she'd been capable of deceiving *him*, how could they trust her? Though Lucas seemed to know what he was doing; instinctively, Jess felt that she could trust him. Unless that was all part of being attracted to him, and her instincts were letting her down.

Nat's car set off, with Sam and Carolyn, and Jess followed Lucas along a narrow path round the back of the cottage. 'Where does this come out?'

'At Pike's back door. This would have been an estate worker's cottage or something.'

Already Jess could see a substantial Victorian house in the distance, across a vast area of smooth green lawn. 'Will anyone see us coming, as we get nearer?' Because Lucas was making no pretence at concealment.

'That's okay.'

'You're expected — but what about me?'

'Yeah, we could try disguising you as a small tree or a flowering shrub? No, I've thought of that. If he sees you, I'll tell him I've found you and am bringing you in, knowing that's what he would want. Top marks for initiative.'

'But I'm walking along freely and willingly?'

'Obviously I've handled it so cleverly that you haven't suspected a thing.'

'Hmm. Why didn't he take us in the first place? He could have had us knocked out, bundled us all into my Dad's car, and sent us all over the cliff together.'

'If he'd ordered *that*, you'd have been finished off before the cliff. No chance of survival. No, he was prioritising, I would think. Leo Dryden and the goods first. Knowing that his workforce would find you when required, without too much trouble.'

Jess tried to hide a shudder. 'So what's the plan for once we're inside?'

Lucas grinned. 'A quick check first to make sure the heavies are out of the way, as arranged. Nat's going to text me. Also highly probable that the Boss will have gone to the staffroom with them. Nat knows that too. Pike will want to play them my vid, telling them they'll be rewarded for the part they played. Acting like a general, motivating and praising the troops — and I'm hoping he'll spin it out, loving his moment of triumph. He's been after your father for a long, long time.'

'You're assuming a lot, aren't you?'

'That's true. It all depends on my reading him right and anticipating what he'll do. But if not, we'll just have to think on our feet.'

'Fine. I can do that.'

He grinned again. 'I'm sure you can. For now, we'll focus on his office. He's almost phobic about security, so the office has a reinforced security door, entry by passcode only. And then there's another room off, like a walk-in mini bank vault. I can't access that, but with any luck, we should have enough time to get into the office before he comes in.'

'You must have the passcode, then?'

'Yes, I have the current one. He wanted me to do something in there last week. No problem if he's changed it since; I can do locks. Part of my CV. In that case, we'll install you inside and I'll wait for him out on the landing.'

'Phone reception okay in there?'

'Yes. And he's keen on luxurious curtains, ideal as a hiding place.'

Jess nodded. Lucas was making everything sound so matter-of-fact. But she was feeling as if none of this was real. Soon, the madness of the last couple of days and the awareness of what had happened to her father would catch up with her. For now, she was responding like a robot. As if some other person was discussing this unreal plan, but she had to go along with it.

Lucas was saying, 'Usually, all the security outside is activated even during the day and whether the Boss is in or not. Any visitors have to report from the security gates and use the intercom. But he's expecting me so he's switched it off.' He glanced at her. 'Just as he would when he was expecting Carolyn.'

'I see. I don't think I want to know too much about Carolyn's activities.'

'Fair enough.'

*Change the subject.* 'It's a lovely house.'

'It should be. He's thrown a lot of money at it, but it's still like a rabbit warren. Knocking a few walls down would have improved things — but, easier for us.' He nodded upwards. 'See, that's his office window, on the first floor. You can just make out the curtains from here. All you have to do is record what he says and keep out of sight.'

'And then what?'

'He'll go into his secure room and start gloating over the bags. He'll be there for a while, happily occupied.'

Jess glanced up at the window. They were almost underneath it now. No nearby drainpipes or handy garden features that could be useful if Lucas had misjudged things and she had to climb down. Just have to hope he was right about all this, then.

Lucas put a finger to his lips. She nodded. How could this ever work? Even though he made it sound so easy. He rounded the corner of the house, and led her through an unassuming back door — which would once have led to the servants' quarters and kitchen, she supposed. Twisting and turning corridors, cupboards and sculleries. Presumably the Boss wasn't too interested in kitchens. But, fair enough, it was his house.

Somewhere, she could hear voices. Smithson Pike talking to his employees? Lucas quickly turned another corner until the voices receded. Probably why they seemed to be taking a roundabout route.

She wondered where Nat and Sam were now. Was there more than one back door? More than likely. Nothing would surprise her in this house. Just as well that the others had Carolyn to direct them. Unless she only knew the direct route to Smithson Pike's bedroom. Jess pulled a face.

Up a stark set of stairs, in keeping with the servants' quarters, through a door, then abruptly into a world of soft carpets and velvet curtains with gilt-framed paintings on the flock-papered walls. One elegant door, however, was ostentatiously out of place, with the keypad proclaiming all too obviously what lay behind it.

Lucas mouthed silently, 'Here goes.' He tapped the code in, turned the handle, and they slid in. 'Obviously I'm still in favour. That's something.'

'Of course you are. You're the golden boy in his eyes.' Jess couldn't prevent a coldness coming into her voice. There was little room to move inside; much of the floorspace was taken up with a large oak desk, and a high-backed leather-covered swivel chair with carved and polished arms.

Lucas said only, 'Okay, go behind the curtains. If I stand over here, he'll have to look away from them to speak to me.'

Jess nodded, stepping behind them. 'Any sign of me?'

'Mm. They don't drape quite like that usually. Move to the right a bit. That's better. Ah! Here's a text from Nat. The Boss has just set off.'

Jess frowned. 'I didn't hear anything.'

'I'm on silent.' He paused. 'Are you sure you're okay with this?'

In spite of everything, Jess almost laughed. 'Too bad if not. I'm here now.'

'Yes. You need to be able to see. No, don't move. I'll make a couple of slits in the curtain. One for you and one for the phone. And the linings. Those okay for you?'

She bent and put one eye to the slit where the phone would be. 'Fine.' Almost reluctantly, she said, 'You've thought of everything.'

He whispered urgently, 'That's it now.'

Jess hadn't heard a thing, but he was right. In less than a minute, she heard the click of the lock opening. She positioned her phone and began recording the unmistakable voice, chilling even when expressing approval. 'Lucas! Well done. The world is well rid of that deceitful worm. The one thing I cannot, *cannot*, stand, is disloyalty — and Leo Dryden found that out to his cost. He's paid the ultimate price.'

'I don't know how he ever thought he could get away with it,' Lucas said. 'Not against you.'

'He was always a gifted crook, certainly, but greed got the better of him. Together with pride and arrogance.'

Through the slit level with her eyes,

Jess could see him crossing the room, leaning heavily on his stick. Lowering himself into his swivel chair with his back to her. But as he turned to face Lucas, on the other side of the desk, his profile was in view. His face was pale and there was sweat on his forehead. Excitement, no doubt, Jess thought.

She was filled with revulsion for him. Of course he had been angry on discovering Leo Dryden's betrayal; she could understand that. But exulting like this after seeing the film of her father's supposed death; that was horrible. She could well believe that he would not rest until he had silenced the witnesses at the quarry.

Lucas was saying, 'Clever in a way, though, I suppose. Recognising a superior ability in you, his boss, in organising the robberies so efficiently — and then spotting the opportunity for benefiting from that himself.'

'Yes. I spotted his talents from the first. I only employ people with the abilities I need. But he slipped up, of course, in having to involve the other employees in his group — then quickly becoming very unwilling to share the gains with them. He made everything too complicated, and in the process, left a glaring trail behind him.'

All true, as Jess knew. But this was hardly useful for gaining a conviction, for either Smithson Pike or her father — because she would have to accept that some of her evidence she gained here would probably be used to convict him too. Also, so far, Smithson Pike was only using language that could have applied to any business transaction. Not much help.

'You've got me intrigued, you know,' Lucas said. 'Where did this haul come from? And what is it, exactly?'

There was a silence. Jess held her breath. Was Pike becoming suspicious? She looked though the eye slit and saw him leaning back in his chair, gently rubbing his hands together while he gazed up at the white plaster leaves and flowers of the ceiling cornice.

'Yes,' he said at last. 'I wouldn't tell everyone. Make no mistake about that. But I will tell you. You have proved your worth, working faithfully for me while convincing Dryden that you were working for him. Observing his younger daughter and passing on all that information about her whereabouts and movements — to both of us.'

'Engineering her movements, as often as not,' Lucas said. His voice was cold and objective.

Jess shivered. He sounded like a completely different person.

Lucas continued, 'Making sure that she — and Oliver — ended up renting flats owned by Leo. And for Sam to be employed in a business owned by him. A business set up years ago, with your money, of course. A grave mistake on Dryden's part to put that dizzy little girlfriend of his, Claire, into watching Sam too. That almost went very wrong and wrecked everything. He should have trusted me to do the whole thing.'

'Oh, yes. Claire, wasn't it? Could

fancy her myself. Where is she now? What's happened to her?'

'They left her tied up at Nat's house.'

'Not dead, then?'

'No.' Lucas paused. 'Do you want her to be?' That chilling voice again. No wonder Pike trusted him so implicitly.

Pike was nodding. 'I think so. Rather a waste, but better that way. No body though. Better for her to disappear altogether.'

'That's fine. I'll see to it.'

Smithson Pike gave a satisfied laugh. 'That's exactly what I mean about you, Lucas. If I give you a task, I know you'll handle it. So, yes, I will answer your question. You may well have heard about this robbery. It comes up on internet searches of the most successful heists if you look hard enough.'

Jess listened while he helpfully outlined all the details of how he had planned and expedited the robbery of a certain bank vault in the West End. 'You'll have heard of the Baker Street bank vault robbery? Got a lot of publicity. Mine was much more discreet. Although, equally, the owners of the document boxes wanted only to avoid publicity and the whole thing was forgotten very quickly. Which was just how I liked it, too. The police gave up on it in a matter of months.'

Jess was almost forgetting to breathe. Lucas was leaning forward, his hands on the far edge of the desk, nodding his admiration.

Pike sighed, as if he had been reliving all the excitement of his youthful triumph and was sorry that his story was over. 'There, that's how it was. And I'm glad you asked me, because there's something else. You saw how easily Leo Dryden was deceived by the report of my supposed death? Well, if he had actually waited a little longer, he may well have achieved the safety he craved.'

Lucas was looking concerned. 'What do you mean?'

'I'm dying. No, no platitudes, please. You're a bright lad; you've been with me for some time now. You've witnessed my deterioration.'

'I didn't want to believe it,' Lucas said in a low voice.

'Comes to all of us. You remind me so much of myself at your age. I have no family that I care to recognise. My cousin's children are worthless idiots. There's no one else. There's only you who I care about at all — and Carolyn.' He nodded, slowly. 'So I have left everything I have to you — and a proportion to her.' He paused. He seemed to be gasping for breath.

'Are you all right?' Lucas stood up.

'Tablets; top right-hand drawer.'

Jess tensed. Lucas seemed to be taking a long time in the drawer. What would happen if he didn't produce them? Would it save everyone a great deal of trouble? *No, don't even think it.*

She turned her head slightly. Had that been a faint clicking sound from the door? As if the keypad had been activated, maybe? But neither Pike nor Lucas seemed to have noticed. She must have imagined it.

'Quickly,' Smithson Pike barked, his voice strangled. 'Thank you. That's better.' Jess could hear nothing for a few moments but the heaviness of his breathing, until it gradually calmed to a more normal rate. 'I had a bit of an odd turn earlier; that's why I came back here instead of overseeing Leo's death as planned. But knowing he was in good hands.'

Lucas said, 'I can't tell you how much I appreciate this. Your generosity.'

'Don't bother. Words mean nothing. You're so like me, remember? So I know when I hear emptiness. No need. I know what's going on inside your head. But you have just proved that all my instincts were right. You could have let me die then, after what I'd just told you. But you didn't.'

'Of course not.'

'No *of course* about it. I'll guarantee that you thought of it.'

'Yes.' Lucas sounded cautious, and who could blame him?

Smithson Pike laughed. 'Now. Back

to business. There's Leo's bimbo of a girlfriend, Claire, to be dealt with; and those other three. Loose ends, that's all. But it will be easy to track them down and eliminate them. Amateurs, all three of them. They have no idea what they've got into, and aren't taking it seriously. They will soon learn their mistake.' He laughed again. 'Tell you what, we can throw the task open to all of you. Make a bit of a contest of it. With a suitable reward to spice things up.'

Jess felt as if she could explode with fury. She had to clench her hands and every muscle she could think of to prevent herself leaping out and confronting him. How dare he? Playing with people's lives like this? And hers in particular. *No, do it the way Lucas had advised, the sensible way.* The phone was still on. She had that admission on record too now.

'Good idea,' Lucas said. He stopped, as if thinking. 'But — one thing. Those two girls are Carolyn's daughters. How will she feel about this?'

'See what you mean. A bit unfortunate, but can't be helped. And she doesn't need to know about it. Discretion; we'll add that to the instructions. Seriously, though, they know far too much. You don't want them interfering — '

The door was flung open.

# 22

Carolyn burst into the room. She was the explosion of rage that her daughter was suppressing. 'What are you talking about? How dare you! As if my daughters don't matter. Well, to you, I don't suppose they do. Why should they?'

Pike reeled backwards, initially shocked — but rallied in moments. 'Now, my dear, you have to understand — '

'Don't you *my dear* me.'

He ignored her. 'You weren't meant to hear this conversation.'

'I'll bet I wasn't.'

'Because it was irrelevant. You have been around me and close to me for long enough by now to realise that my instructions to my employees rarely reflect my true feelings. And for you to know how I can be with the people I really care about.'

Carolyn made a dismissive noise. Jess

was filled with a reluctant admiration for her. She had to be putting herself in danger, and yet she didn't seem to care.

Pike's voice was soft and persuasive. 'You know how much you mean to me. And how much we mean to each other.'

Jess held her breath. *Had* he meant anything to Carolyn?

Carolyn's voice rose. 'No! It's time for the truth. You *never* meant anything to me. It was the only way I could get back at my worthless ex-husband; and, once he had been dealt with by you, gain protection for my youngest child and the two Leo had stolen from me. That mattered more.' She stepped forwards, confronting him. 'Sam means the whole world to me. For years, she's been all I had left. And now you're talking about disposing of her — and Jess too — as if they didn't matter. You scum, I didn't think any man could be worse than Leo — but you are.'

Smithson seemed to be dismissing this as a female tantrum. He reached out to her, still with a placating smile.

Carolyn snatched her arm away. 'Don't touch me!'

And then everything moved so quickly that Jess could hardly keep up. The frail old man suddenly had an arm around Carolyn's neck, twisting her round and gripping her tightly. In spite of her struggles, she was unable to free herself. And with a thrill of horror, Jess saw that he had a knife to her throat.

Lucas said quietly, 'Let her go, Smithson. She's not worth it.'

Jess doubted whether Smithson Pike had even heard him. But from where Lucas was standing, it seemed unlikely that he could do anything to help. Any sudden movement and Pike would have killed Carolyn long before Lucas could reach her.

Jess was behind him, however. And he had no idea she was there. She focused all her attention on the handle of the knife, clearly visible in Pike's thin, veined hand.

Smithson Pike said, bitterly, 'As I told you, betrayal is the one thing, above all others, that I cannot forgive. I should have suspected it. Why would an attractive woman like this fall for an old man like me? Money and power, that's what she was after. But she was good. Oh, yes. She gave a brilliant portrayal of affection. Love, even.' He laughed. 'Strangely enough, this was something Leo Dryden was right about. He always said she was a double-dealing witch, and I chose to ignore him.'

Lucas said, more loudly but his voice still calm, 'I can handle this for you, quickly and cleanly. You don't need to dirty your hands with it.'

'No. This is down to me. My mess, my responsibility. Some things can't be left to the servants. If something matters, I deal with it myself. Always have, always will. And this lady matters.'

Jess felt a thrill of horror. He was actually going to do it. He was going to kill Carolyn right there, in front of them. She couldn't let this happen. Whatever her mother had done or not done. None of that mattered now.

*Focus on the knife*. She put the phone safely in her pocket, leaving her hands free. Cautiously, she slid out from behind the curtains, hoping desperately that Lucas, facing her, would have the presence of mind not to acknowledge her movements, even with his eyes. He merely folded his arms and shrugged, as if in answer to Smithson Pike.

Slowly, silently, one step at a time. She considered how best she could do this. Yes, holding her arm above and behind him and a little to one side. She flexed her fingers. Now.

She went for the knife with one hand, and grabbed at the arm round Carolyn's neck with the other. She had surprise on her side.

He might be old, but he was also incredibly strong. Carolyn, falling forward as she was freed, was also thinking quickly. Grasping one flailing arm and hanging on. Jess threw the knife backwards onto the floor, out of reach. She had no intention of using it by mistake. Now she could concentrate on Pike's left arm, and between them, they were holding him.

Smithson Pike spluttered, 'Lucas! Don't just stand there. Get these harpies off me. Get the gun from my drawer.'

Lucas obeyed, sliding the drawer open again and pointing the pistol at the struggling group.

'See? Now get off me.'

'No,' Lucas said. 'All of you, stay where you are.'

'What's the matter with you? This woman has betrayed me. Surely you can see that?'

'I can see everything, Smithson, all too clearly. More so than you. The thing is — ' Lucas paused, stepping closer and levelling the gun so that it pointed only at Pike. 'I'm afraid Carolyn isn't the only one who has deceived you. I have too. From the very beginning.'

Smithson Pike became still. Jess felt his arm go limp in her hands. 'What? What do you mean? You're like a son to me. I told you so. You're like me. Two peas in a pod.'

'No, I'm not, and I never have been. I've been working undercover, to bring you to justice. Long overdue. And now, with the help of these two, I have all the evidence I need.'

Smithson Pike's face became beetroot red, suffused with blood. Before just as quickly, becoming deathly white. He spluttered something, but the words would not emerge from his mouth.

Abruptly, Jess and her mother were unable to hold his weight. A gurgling noise came from his throat as he slumped to the floor.

Carolyn swiftly knelt beside him, seeking a pulse in his neck, putting a hand in front of his open mouth. She looked up at the other two. 'I think he's dead.'

# 23

Sam looked amazing in a slender fountain of white satin, starflowers in her blonde hair. She said, 'Thanks, Jess. Thank you so much for agreeing to do this.'

Jess grinned. 'I wouldn't have missed it.' She stooped to rearrange the dress slightly. Glancing up at her sister, she surprised a strangely mischievous smile on Sam's face, as if Sam was brimming over with a secret joke. No, must be imagining things. This was a day for smiling. 'Ready, Sam?'

No father to take her down the central aisle in the spacious Georgian mansion in the park. He had hardly begun his sentence. No brother, either; poor confused Oliver had not survived the fall into the quarry. Carolyn, sedate in lilac silk, with graceful feathers adorning her hat, took Sam's arm.

Jess thought that Sam so deserved

this happiness. She and Nat made a lovely couple, and how lucky they all were to have survived the events of over a year ago to enjoy this day.

There were few friends from the bride's side, with moving house too often and too swiftly, and no relatives either. But Nat had more than made up for it. A roomful of people who were strangers to the Dryden family, but all so willing to share in the joy of the occasion. Jess smiled round at them, pacing with unaccustomed dignity in the floor-length dusty pink gown.

She gasped. There was one face she did know, smiling back. She missed her step, struggled to recover. Lucas. What on earth was he doing here? Of course. No wonder Sam had been so happily secretive.

An echo of that happiness was welling within her as she passed him. Was he with anyone? Had his invitation said 'and guest'? No, surely not; because Sam would have known and would have broken it to her gently.

Calm down. You're Chief Bridesmaid. You're here to support the bride. Lucas, she thought sternly, could be dealt with later. All this time and never a word.

Nat turned as they reached the front and Jess felt a pang in her heart, seeing the look that passed between bride and groom. She moved forward to take Sam's bouquet and arrange her train again. There was something just so beautiful that existed between them. She sat down on the front row with the other bridesmaids.

Lucas had seemed pleased to see her. But where had he been all these months? Concentrate. Rings, vows, register. Retracing their steps in time to the joyful wedding march. This time, she would stare straight ahead. At the last moment, her eyes slid to the left, and he was still grinning at her as if he had read her mind and was amused by it — and she just had to laugh back somehow. But once past him, she didn't look round.

Fortunately, she was needed for the

photographs. More assiduous arranging of fabric, more than was necessary. Quite a while before a moment came when there was nothing at all for the Chief Bridesmaid to do. Be sociable. Circulate. Somebody was saying, 'A beautiful venue. Is the bride from Leeds too?'

'Yes,' Jess said. 'We were both born here.' *If only you knew.* But the lady in the blue-green dress seemed satisfied.

'And the rest,' Lucas murmured, from behind her.

'I know.'

'Hello, Jess. Good to see you again.'

She breathed in, slowly. Be calm. 'You too.' And promptly forgetting the good intention as soon as it was formed, 'What happened to you? You just melted away.'

'I thought it seemed best.'

What? Best for who? Keep things cool. 'I was expecting to hear from you. I mean, I thought I would be called on to give evidence. But I never even saw it mentioned in the media.'

'No. Pike died of natural causes and his criminal activities died with him. No point in going through the circus of court action. Might have compromised the department, anyway.'

Her eyes widened. She said indignantly, 'So that recording I made — and sweated over? It wasn't even necessary?'

'Oh, I wouldn't say that. It clarified a few things for my unit.'

'But his death? Didn't the shock of everything we did and said contribute to that?'

'More than likely. But he was dying anyway. And there's no need to feel any guilt about it. He would have had you killed.'

'I know. I don't. But because I was expecting to give some kind of evidence to somebody — I thought that meant I would see you again.'

'Ah, I see.' He paused. 'I didn't think you'd want me around.'

'What? For someone so good at an incredibly difficult job — ' She bit her lip. She wanted to say, *I can't believe you got that so wrong.* She said carefully, 'I don't suppose, having a job like that, you can afford to get entangled with anyone. You can only have a relationship when it's part of your work. Like seeing Sam was.' She felt a pang of jealousy. How many other women had he been instructed to get close to?

'True, I suppose. You have to do things that can be — regrettable. But, Jess, I'm not doing that job anymore. I told you, remember?'

'I didn't know whether to believe you. I thought I would wait and see. And then nothing happened.' If true, why had he not made some effort to contact her? A text checking if she was okay? A Facebook message?

'Leaving was a longer process than I expected. More loose ends to tie up.'

'I see.' Was this going anywhere? Jess didn't know. She sighed. 'Well, I'd better carry on with my duties.' She added unnecessarily, 'I have to look after the bride.'

320

Lucas laughed. 'I think she has her new husband to look after her now.' He took her hand in his. 'I would never suggest that you need someone to look after you. But I'd like to be on hand — just in case you should get involved in any other criminal conspiracies.'

Jess laughed too. 'I've no intention of doing anything of the sort. But you're welcome to stick around, just to make sure.' For one wild, heady moment, she thought he might be about to kiss her. They stared into each other's eyes.

And then he *was* kissing her, and the crowd and the murmur of voices around them became a distant blur.

We do hope that you have enjoyed reading this large print book.

Did you know that all of our titles are available for purchase?

We publish a wide range of high quality large print books including:
**Romances, Mysteries, Classics**
**General Fiction**
**Non Fiction and Westerns**

Special interest titles available in large print are:
**The Little Oxford Dictionary**
**Music Book, Song Book**
**Hymn Book, Service Book**

Also available from us courtesy of Oxford University Press:
**Young Readers' Dictionary**
**(large print edition)**
**Young Readers' Thesaurus**
**(large print edition)**

For further information or a free brochure, please contact us at:
**Ulverscroft Large Print Books Ltd.,**
**The Green, Bradgate Road, Anstey,**
**Leicester, LE7 7FU, England.**
**Tel:** (00 44) **0116 236 4325**
**Fax:** (00 44) **0116 234 0205**